THE PACIFIC BILLIONAIRE VINTNER

TONI KENYON

apeople
Publishing

Published by:

Apeople Publishing

Copyright © 2017 by Toni Kenyon

All rights reserved.

ISBN: 978-0-9941488-2-7

The Pacific Billionaire Vintner is a work of fiction. Names, characters, places, and incidents are the products of the author's imagination or are used fictitiously. Any resemblance to actual events, locales, or persons, living or dead, is entirely coincidental.

For Kevin - A great love

INTRODUCTION

Author note: I live in New Zealand and I write in British English. Here in New Zealand we have **footpaths** not sidewalks and **taps** not faucets. We talk about the flavour of ice cream and the colour of the sky. I apologise in advance if you find any of our idiosyncrasies confusing and I hope you enjoy your visit to my homeland. Feel free to email me if there's something you need me to explain—I'll do my best and be happy to oblige.

Can two fractured hearts come together to create one great love?

Billionaire Vintner, Harry Pearson returns from overseas to his family's vineyard on Hauraki Island in New Zealand with plans to develop the estate into the finest vineyard complex in the country—and bring some much needed prosperity to the Island. Emotionally traumatised from an affair gone astray and struggling with the aftermath of his late father's drinking, womanising and disastrous business deals, he vows he will never love again.

Grace Richards wants out of New Zealand and away from Hauraki Island. After a stressful stint at university studying commerce, she's hiding out and licking her wounds in the family bach at tranquil, Spindle Bay. Grace decides the only way forward with her life is to follow her dream and study photography in Europe. All she needs now is to make enough money to get on the plane and leave the painful past behind her.

When the lure of big money means that Grace ends up working as Harry's PA she struggles to keep the relationship professional. What Harry doesn't count on is Grace's fiery passion for Hauraki Island reigniting his capacity to open his heart to the possibility of love.

Can Harry convince Grace to let go of her dream to escape and create a life with him as head of the Pearson dynasty?

CHAPTER 1

H **arry**
    I'd come home to the island of my childhood and brought with me a dark cloud of despair. I stood on the verandah, staring out across the vast, familiar track of lush green vines in their regimented rows and on to the view of Auckland city beyond the Hauraki Gulf.

I was back in New Zealand because of my lineage and the promise to my mother that I would repair the damage done by my father. Given the ability to make my own decisions about my future, I would have stayed in Italy. But my mother, Kathryn needed me and I owed her and my family a debt of honour.

Unlike the drunken bastard that was my father, I held the good name of the family at my heart. I would do whatever was necessary to ensure that my mother went to her grave knowing that all her heartache and good work would not be lost.

Kathryn assured me I was heartsick and that a good season of work in amongst the vines would heal my pain. I simply raged with anger every time I thought about the woman who had claimed to be my girlfriend.

Ex-girlfriend, I reminded myself.

Perhaps being back here in my hometown would be the healing tonic needed to get over the betrayal.

I swore that no woman would ever treat me that way again. I'd made the mistake of believing I could have a cut and dried business arrangement with a woman and it had gone astray.

The pain at the memory of seeing her with another man rose like bile in my throat. I understood business. Simple transactions. There was recourse if one side of the contract was broken. Not so with women, it seemed.

I sipped wine from the glass in my hand. The soft, fruity bouquet of the Merlot had been expertly blended and the taste exploded in my mouth.

My family had been blending our wines for many years now and I felt more of a pull to Hauraki Island as a result of the bouquet of the wine. I held the glass aloft and looked at the light as it fractured through the red liquid. This product would always be responsible for ensuring my return to the Island and its vines. I was a Pearson and the nectar of the grape—another product of the land—ran strong in my blood, as it had for generations of my family before me.

I would take mother's advice and throw myself into my work. I had returned from my extended fact finding mission in Italy with not only the pain of betrayal, but also with great plans to build wine caves to house our vast supply of ageing vintages. We produced medal winning wines; we had tourists galore already converging on the island, but I also wanted to turn our estate into the number one place to be and to be seen.

To do that I'd had to instigate changes that weren't popular with a fair number of the current staff. I knew everyone was talking behind my back. I didn't give a shit. I wasn't here to be Mr Popularity—I'd never been Mr Popularity and I was used to having to clean up my late father's cockups. I was here to make sure that the Pearson name stayed at the forefront of everyone's mind. That our wines continued to grace the finest eating establishments in the world and that our vineyard became the number one attraction in the area.

If that made me Mr McNasty then I didn't care. I had a vision, the drive to see it through to fruition and nothing would get in my way.

*G*race
    I stared at the extended line of people waiting to be seated for lunch and wondered how much longer I could stand working at the Pearson's vineyard restaurant.

Granted, many would have been happy to exchange their position with mine. The vineyard restaurant occupied a premier position on Hauraki Island. Situated on one of the island's many rugged headlands and with a spectacular view of the Hauraki Gulf and Auckland city.

All I could do was look at the city with something that amounted to loathing.

Sure, I could be over there, working the same soul-destroying job in Queen Street, or at one of the trendy cafes that had sprung up around the city, but the idea of travelling back and forth every day on the ferry did not appeal.

Saving money to escape New Zealand and go overseas did appeal and that's how I found myself bunking in at my parents summer holiday home on the shores of Spindle Bay. Broken and unable to complete a commerce degree that I didn't want to start in the first place, I'd had to go cap-in-hand to my parents. The bach came with a self-imposed time limit. Six months I'd told them was all I needed and then I'd move on.

I'd already been here for four months—working as hard as I could to amass enough money to make a break for Europe.

The family bach was a tiny 1920's board and batten lean-to building and one of the few that had survived the onslaught of the Island becoming an outer suburb of Auckland city. The original building had retained its holiday home charm. The Island had always been my sanctuary—but now, for reasons I couldn't fathom—I found the once appealing isolation somewhat overpowering.

"Grace, table 83," the shrill shout of Kathryn Pearson cut into my meandering thoughts. I nodded an acknowledgment and went to clear the plates and remaining food from the large, outdoor wooden table, before the local bird life swooped in to clean up the leftovers.

I found it difficult to understand the enthusiasm of the tourists that I served daily when my own thoughts about my home country were in a state of disarray.

Day in and day out there appeared to be an unwavering stream of nationalities coming through the establishment.

As I cleared the table, I couldn't help staring across the expanse of almost green water. Today's wind blew the ocean into frothing white caps and forced the Island's ferries to travel close to the shore. I spent far too much time looking out at the city and its tall silver buildings that shimmered in the afternoon sun. I often wondered about the occupants of those buildings and whether they were happy. Ever since I'd spent long childhood holidays here on the Island, I'd had a love-hate relationship with the city of Auckland. At present we had become somewhat disaffected lovers and I was almost grateful for failing my commerce degree. Being holed up in a cubicle in one of the buildings that I watched each day had never appealed to me.

The table cleared. My senses were again assaulted by the ringing of the bell to indicate that food was ready for serving.

Kathryn Pearson ran a tight ship and there was little time for sitting with my own thoughts while I moved food from kitchen to table and back again. This time I delivered an aromatic beef stew that had been laced with plenty of red wine, to a large, middle aged man who looked as if he should have been eating the beetroot salad that his gaunt wife had ordered.

I'd been around the Island long enough to remember when the vine covered hillsides that surrounded me were no more than grassy paddocks.

The Pearson family had owned large tracts of land on the Island for as long as there had been records kept of land ownership. Generations ago they were farming folk, but latterly the family had turned their attention to wine making. They continued to acquire large portions of land to either develop or convert to vineyards.

Rumour had it that the Pearson family had bought up this particular portion of land when I was a little over four years old—bailing out the land owner who had tried unsuccessfully to make a go of farming the harsh land on the hill.

The locals knew that the most recent old man Pearson was a drunk and a gambler who had spent most of his time in the whore houses down on the waterfront in Auckland city. Kathryn, his stoic wife had managed the business and the land and kept the family from bankruptcy on many occasions.

It was only since the latest generation of Pearson men had taken control of the vineyard after the passing of their father that the business had again begun to flourish.

Despite their patriarch's propensity for more than wine, the family were notorious for their cut-throat tactics. As other vineyards in the area had tried to emulate their success and then struck trouble, the Pearson family had swooped in and snapped them up. The latest generation of Pearson's thus found themselves with a dynastic monopoly and an extraordinary amount of money at their disposal.

All the years I'd been coming to the Island, I tried to stay out of local politics. My one exception had been doing some photography work for Fish & Bird, the local wildlife conservation group. In the last four months, I'd done quite a bit of work for them. The creative photography kept me sane as one day meshed into another.

Swathes of tourists, not unlike the two I'd just delivered lunch, visited the Island on a daily basis. They came to experience its quaint tourist spots and then they stopped in at Pearson's Vineyard for lunch. Most enjoyed the vineyard's barrel tasting tour before heading for the ferry with large orders of the vineyard's wines in hand.

I spent eight hours a day under the eagle eye of Kathryn Pearson, the Matriarch of the family. She didn't miss a single thing. Every tea-light had to sit right in the centre of every barrel that lined the edge of the restaurant walls. Woe betide me if a single piece of cutlery was out of alignment before the guests sat down to lunch.

Pushing a stray lock of my long, blonde hair back behind my ear, I cursed the size of my ample hips as I tried to squeeze myself between a table and another wine barrel. Only two more months of this, I reminded myself, until I'd have enough money put aside to take up the challenge of studying overseas. I could finally get away from this damn Island and Auckland and fulfil my dream of travelling across Europe.

How I'd managed to allow my parents to shoe horn me into a commerce degree I'd never know.

I'd taken this job because it paid two dollars an hour more than any other job on the Island. That was because no-one wanted to work for the Pearson family or Kathryn. She had a reputation for driving her staff hard. But I didn't care about that, all I cared about was making sure that I had enough money to get to Europe. From there, I could take up my photography studies. I could stand a few months of hard work if it meant I could achieve my goal and find a way to the riches of historical Europe.

Kathryn did what she did well and she prided herself on the fact that the Pearson name was synonymous with quality. The family's recent success had seen off the local Island competition and the Pearson's had weathered many recessions. But now, they were also seeing the added benefits of escalating land prices in the Auckland area. This increased their stronghold, as the city's wealthy looked to make Hauraki Island their home.

A surge in recent competition throughout the rest of the country meant that Kathryn and her sons had redoubled their efforts. They worked hard to ensure that their wines maintained their world-wide status.

There was also the Harry Pearson factor to take into consideration. The eldest Pearson son had returned from an extended period in Italy with grand ideas. I worked hard to stay under everyone's radar. I didn't want any trouble. I came to work and I did my job and I went home to my beach side sanctuary.

Harry it seemed, had taken the entire estate by the scruff of the neck and given it a great big shake up. A shake up that some of the regular staff didn't survive. Another reason to make sure that I kept my mouth shut and stayed out of the limelight.

I couldn't understand why anyone would come home to New Zealand when they had the chance to live in Italy—but then I guess I wasn't the head of a dynasty and I didn't have the weight of expectation of someone like Kathryn bearing down on me.

My parents lived in the outer suburbs of Auckland—where they had for most of my life. They loved the Island, but not so much now that it had itself become an outer suburb of the sprawling city.

After my spectacular university and relationship failure, tucking me away from friends and family at the Island seemed like a sensible solution to them.

I wasn't in any kind of position or state of mind to argue. I was grateful for the solitude and the chance to hide here and lick my wounds.

So now, I found myself alone and trying to follow my artistic dreams. Despite my parents' disappointment, I guessed they were both happy that I'd made the decision to go over to Europe to expand my personal horizons. Without their support in the form of the bach at Spindle Bay, there was no way that I'd be standing here now.

The sight of Harry Pearson caught my eye as he approached the restaurant. He had arrived home one mean, angry son-of-a-bitch. 6′2 of pure panty-wetting gorgeousness. His masculine beauty hadn't been lost on my eye and, frankly, that scared the living shit out of me.

I was a photographer.

Beauty in all its forms inspired me. I didn't need the complication of inspiration in the form of Harry David Pearson.

The barrel tasting tour had been one of a number of new initiatives that Harry had spearheaded. I tried to stay well away from him. The way my body reacted when he was around disturbed me more than anything else. Thankfully, he didn't venture often to the restaurant, leaving the running of the catering operation in the more than capable hands of his mother.

"Grace," the siren call of Kathryn cut through the echo of knives and forks on porcelain, "over here, please." She was all please and thank you and politeness, but lord help me if I didn't run the second that Kathryn called. I pulled my golden apron straight over my regulation vineyard t-shirt and denim shorts and made my way at pace toward the woman who would rule my life for the next few months.

I swear I must have blinked, he came out of nowhere, in fact, I didn't even see where he'd come from but I felt him. I walked at speed, straight into the solid wall of muscle that was Harry Pearson. Not only did I knock the wind out of myself, but I ended up flat on my arse at his feet.

"It's nice to meet you, Grace. Can I help you off the floor?" I looked up, ready to give the belligerent bastard a piece of my mind, but all I could see was an outstretched hand and beyond that a sculptured jaw that sported a hint of five o'clock shadow and a shade of a smile.

At the sound of my name, my knees refused to co-operate and I feared I'd be stuck down here for the rest of the afternoon. If the sensual tone of his voice could do that to me, I thought, what the hell would taking his hand do?

CHAPTER 2

*H*arry

I may have had a vision, but I still needed assistance to turn that vision into reality. The locals around here didn't take too kindly to change.

I had been researching the major earthworks required to build my wine caves.

We owned enough land either side of the main vineyard to ensure that I could complete the earthworks without getting tangled up in unnecessary red tape with neighbours.

I'd managed to keep things relatively quiet, until the day that the large earthmoving machinery had moved in.

A few local feathers had been ruffled—but I'd been expecting that. What I hadn't expected was the resistance I would get from my three younger brothers.

Ben, Nicholas and Sebastian were inclined to sit back and let me run the vineyard with mother the way that the two of us thought fit. They hadn't yet had the experience of travelling extensively like me although they had all spent considerable time in Switzerland. Our final gap years were spent in Europe.

Still, they had been schooled in the intricacies of business management and hospitality in some of the best institutions the world had to offer—but the complicated ins and outs of expansions eluded them.

None of my brothers were the best pick to assist me with this project. That had been evident on the day the earth moving equipment had arrived. Seb mouthed off at one of the protestors from Fish & Bird and all hell broke out.

A fist fight ensued and it was only due to some fast talking by me that we didn't end up down the road providing the lone sergeant who ran the Island station with a statement.

The hefty contribution that I made to the Island's Friday night teen youth programme probably helped.

No.

I needed someone who would take direction from me and none of my three siblings would bend—we were all as stubborn and hot-headed as each other. That Pearson stubborn streak had been passed to us by our mother—without it she'd have collapsed under the pressure of living with my father years ago.

Kathryn had stood, one hundred percent behind my expansion ideas, so now I found myself in her domain, looking for someone to help me with the management of the project. I knew Kathryn had a tight reign on the staff and I needed someone quickly to assist me. I didn't have the time or the inclination to go through the process of advertising for someone to fill the position.

On my return I'd earned a reputation as a hatchet man and now only good, keen workers remained on site. I was certain that Kathryn would be able to spare me someone and pick herself up a replacement in no time at all. We were paying above the local rate, so there was still no shortage of people applying for positions on our staff.

We paid well—but we expected one hundred and fifty

percent from our staff—like we expected one hundred and fifty percent from ourselves.

As I made my way through the line of tour buses to the entrance of the restaurant, I could hear the sound of voices coming from the direction of the luncheon area. After they'd eaten, our guests would go on a tour of the vineyard and then return to the tasting rooms to further sample our wines. Their day would finish with a visit to the shop where we would sell them plenty of wine to take back to the city via the local ferry. A few might stay at the guest houses scattered around the island, but the majority came to us from Auckland and the larger suburbs beyond.

It had occurred to me that a large accommodation wing was one of the projects that we should be looking into for future expansion.

As I approached Kathryn's seat of power, I was assaulted by the scent of roast meat and my stomach grumbled, reminding me that I hadn't attended to its needs this afternoon. I'd pick something up from the kitchen once I'd seen Kathryn. It took a few moments for my eyes to adjust to the muted light of the restaurant. The inside portion had been built to resemble an old underground cave. Barrels lined the walls and the muted light made it hard for my eyes to adjust from the bright daylight coming in from the outside courtyard.

Light from the hundreds of candles that lined the walls flickered over the rough, cave-like walls and together with the strings of tiny light bulbs strung on the ceiling the room had a warm, womb-like feel.

It was the environment that I wanted to create underground and hence the large earthmoving machinery that sat outside the vineyard gate.

I scanned the circular tables and estimated that there must have been around eighty people in for lunch today.

I spied the white crest of Kathryn's hair, pulled back in the familiar bun that she wore at the nape of her neck when she worked. She stood over on the other side of the space and I picked my way around the edge of the tables to get to her, avoiding waiting staff and tourists alike.

Mother spotted me before I was half-way across the room and issued a welcome, beaming smile.

"We don't normally have the pleasure of your company in here," she said as I kissed her on each cheek in greeting, a habit that I'd picked up while away and one that she seemed to enjoy. "I'm glad to see that you've stopped moping around the estate and you've decided to turn your mind to some work."

I let the gentle criticism go. Mother had become a power-house since the passing of my father more than five years ago. The estate had begun to flourish under our careful management.

Kathryn straightened her apron and issued an order to a passing staff member. The young girl scurried away to clear a table that had been left by a party of four.

Mother turned her attention back to me. "Seb tells me that there was an altercation at the gate this morning over the machinery."

My hackles rose. My youngest brother could do no wrong in my mother's eyes. "Did he also mention that it took a hefty contribution to the youth scheme to make the problem go away?"

Kathryn eyed me in the way she'd just eyed the errant staff member, "You know your brother just needs some responsibility."

"I can't have him working on this project with me. It's too sensitive. He's a hot head and he'll get us closed down before I even start digging the first cave."

We'd had this discussion before today, but I could forgive my mother for pushing Seb forward.

"You know I'm not going to be here forever—"

I cut mother off. "You'll die with your apron on and you're going to be around for at least another two decades, so don't start that with me."

"I only want the best for my boys. All of my boys," she said, the emphasis on the word all.

I hadn't come here to discuss Seb and his wild ways. He only got away with being a wild child because his surname was Pearson. We'd bailed him out of more scrapes than the rest of us put together and that was saying something.

"I need some help," I said in an attempt to change the subject, "and Seb can't help me with this," I said again casting my eye across the room and looking to see how many staff mother had on the floor.

"You will find him something?"

"Of course," anything to get what I needed today. I'd happily put Seb on a plane back to Switzerland if need be, but I could discuss that with mother later. For now I needed someone to assist me managing the site and, more than anything else, managing the locals.

"What kind of help?"

"I need an assistant. Someone who's not afraid of hard work and someone who can pacify Fish & Bird. I'm going to need someone who's not afraid to get their hands dirty, but who has enough brains to be able to think themselves. You got anyone who meets those criteria that you're willing to abandon into my care?"

Mother's staff looked like little worker bees buzzing around the restaurant interior in their regulation black t-shirts and gold wine aprons emblazoned with the vineyard's logo. The only concession to individuality was their choice of denim—jeans or shorts—but the majority chose to wear denim shorts. Mother ruled across them all from her standing desk beside the bar. She'd insisted when the alterations were made to turn the restaurant into a replica wine cave that she would walk the floor with her workers. She wore the exact same uniform, the only recognition of her authority being that she didn't wear the vineyard's gold apron and her jeans were designer. I noted with pride that today she wore one of the pairs I'd brought back myself from Italy. Kathryn met every tourist personally as they entered the restaurant and welcomed them to the land that had housed our family for many years.

I knew that one day, as the eldest son, I would need someone by my side who could take on the role that mother took on when she married my father. My parents marriage may have been troublesome and haunted by my father's dependance on alcohol, but they both had shared a great love of wine and the land and the grapes that they grew.

Even throughout the turbulent years of my father's affairs, drunkenness and out-of-control behaviour they had still managed a dynasty together.

Whenever I looked at the graceful woman that was Kathryn, I despaired that I would ever meet a woman who could follow in her footsteps.

Bitter bile filled my mouth as I thought about my last experience in Italy. Never again would a woman treat me that way. I looked in awe at my mother—she'd put up with such abhorrent behaviour with my father for such a long time. No wonder, she remained so protective of Seb.

"An assistant," Kathryn said as she arched a perfect brow and then scanned the room. "I have the perfect person for you. Ah, there she is." Kathryn gave me a wry smile and I had a fleeting feeling that she may have been up to no good. "Grace, over here please."

"Excuse me, Mr Pearson," another member of the waiting

staff asked me to move aside so he could carry through a large armful of plates. As I moved out of his way, I walked straight into someone warm, soft and curvaceous.

"Your new assistant, Grace," Kathryn whispered in my ear as I looked down into eyes that were the same vivid green as the leaves on the vines in the valley.

Instinctively, I held out my hand to help the young lady to her feet. There was something about Grace that brought out all my protective instincts. "It's nice to meet you, Grace. Can I help you off the floor?"

CHAPTER 3

*G*race

As Harry took my hand and assisted me from the floor, a bolt of pure lust lodged itself in my stomach. My mouth went dry and my heart hammered in my chest. My body responded as if I'd run a marathon, not simply walked from one side of the room to the other.

For some strange reason, I didn't want to let go of his hand. He held me, mesmerised with the energy flowing from his body and captivated in the scrutiny of his dark blue eyes.

When I did eventually regain control of my limbs, I found myself tucking an escaped tendril of my blonde hair behind my ear and smoothing my apron over shorts that suddenly felt far too revealing.

Kathryn broke the strange silence that had descended over us and said, turning her attention on me, "My son needs an assistant to help him with a sensitive project and I've recommended you."

I wasn't sure if I was hearing her right. She was sending me off to work with the man who had single-handedly pissed off the entire workforce on the estate.

"B-but I have diners to look after. Tables to clear," I stammered.

"The meal's almost complete," Kathryn said, "I'll look after your tables or arrange for someone else to cover them. Do not fret."

"No, I'm sorry," I said "my contract is to work here in the restaurant. I'm not employed to be Mr Pearson's assistant."

I watched as Harry's eyes darkened and his lips took on a firm line. From what I understood from the remaining staff, Harry Pearson was used to getting his own way. From the stories I'd heard about the family over the years, I could see the set of his jaw meant that he too had the same Pearson determination. Woe betide anyone who got in the way of a Pearson man and one of his ideas.

Today, I felt unstoppable.

Besides, I didn't care what Harry Pearson thought of me. I was here for another few weeks and then I'd be gone.

Overseas.

Never to return to this island or this country.

"I'll pay you double the hourly rate Kathryn's paying you." He tipped his head sideways, waiting to see my reaction to his offer.

Double the money.

At that rate I could be on a plane even sooner, or I could take almost double the money with me.

Harry's blue eyes drilled into me and my body responded to the intensity of his gaze. My brain registered the offer of more dollars—but my body registered something quite different. I began to appreciate the tenacity of a Pearson man.

"What exactly does this job involve?" I asked my interest piqued, I couldn't be sure if it was the offer of more dollars per hour, or the carnal call of Harry Pearson's body.

"Helping me with an underground development project,"

he said. "I've come back from Italy with some other ideas as well and I need someone to assist me with the management of construction and the locals. Do you think you're up to that?"

The sound of his voice rolled over me. It had the same soothing effect of listening to the waves rolling over the sand at our waterfront bach in Spindle Bay. I had the strange thought that there could be a few other things I might be up to if Harry asked nicely.

Keep your mind on the goal, a voice in my head reminded me. I was tempted to tell it to go back to where it had come from. Spending time with Harry Pearson before I left the country might take some of the edge off the monotony that I found myself surrounded in at the present time.

"I think I might be able to manage," I said.

I swallowed hard.

All I needed to do was keep my head and I'd be on the plane so much earlier than I'd anticipated with a lot more cash than I'd planned on having.

"I'm glad that's settled then," Kathryn said as she flicked her hands in the direction of us, as if she were shooing away a couple of errant pigeons. "Now off you both go."

I untied my gold apron and handed it to Kathryn. I had the utmost respect for a woman who was never afraid to get her hands dirty and work with her staff. The idea, though, of being seconded to the care of Harry terrified and excited me more than I dared to admit to myself. Not because of his fearsome reputation, but because of the way that my internal temperature gauge had gone from freezing to boiling in the few moments that I'd been around the man.

Rumour had it that he had a formidable temper—one not unlike his father. The idea of taking orders from him and the way my body trembled being near him, already had my mind wandering to what he might look like naked.

I mentally slapped myself.

Focus! The voice of reason in my head hissed. That voice of reason had me waiting tables for far too many days a week. It would be well and truly padlocked away when I left New Zealand in a couple of months.

Aside from the warning knell sounding in my head, I couldn't be having out-of-control thoughts about Harry Pearson. If he was anything like his father, he played a rough game with women and tossed them aside when he was done with them.

But you're going away—you'd be tossing him aside. Maybe the voice of reason felt like spicing life up a little as well.

How Kathryn Pearson had remained married to Harry's father for so many years had been the cause of endless speculation around the Island.

To see her, head of this massive enterprise, it was clear to everyone who had controlled this estate. Now, incrementally, control had begun to pass to the next generation of Pearson men. What made me think that Harry Pearson wouldn't be anything other than a replica of his father?

The man even looked the same.

He and his two younger brothers carried the same black hair and blue eyes of their father. Direct descendants of the Pearson line, their genetics appeared unchanged generation after generation. Their father one of a great line of Pearson men who had worked this land over many years and built an empire on this very island.

Sebastian, the youngest Pearson, on the other hand, seemed to have inherited his mother's blonde hair and green eyes.

The odd one out.

He stood like a shining beacon of light against the dark of his three brothers.

Pity, that the light didn't reflect his personality. Seb

caused more trouble than the three Pearson brothers put together—well, that was until Harry returned from Italy and began his crusade to revitalise the old estate.

"Look," Harry said as he placed his hand in the small of my back and began to manoeuvre me around toward the kitchen area of the restaurant. "I haven't eaten and I know you don't get to eat until after the guests have left, so how about we go and pick up a couple of take outs from chef? We can eat them back at my office while I outline to you what the job involves."

My body became hyper-aware of the touch of Harry's hand at my back. My nerves alight with pleasure as we walked towards the kitchen.

Trouble!

The single word came to mind.

Harry Pearson was trouble with a capital T.

I'd never shied away from trouble before and I wasn't about to start now.

CHAPTER 4

Harry

I sat inside my well-appointed portacom, a small modular building that served as my office. I'd removed myself from the rest of the estate while I planned the earthworks and it made sense for me to be as close to site as possible, so I could keep an eye on what was going on.

Now that Grace sat across the other side of my desk, I realised how cramped the space would be with the two of us in here.

Cosy even.

It may well be a portable unit, but I hadn't spared the expense with setting it up comfortably. A large Indian rug adorned the floor bringing some colour to the sparse interior. A walnut desk, Starck chairs and an original Arco floor lamp spanned almost a quarter of the space.

"This is nice," Grace said as I ushered her through the door. Our on-site electrical workers had wired the building and fitted air conditioning. Our carpenters had added a small wooden deck out the front with an arbour so I could sit and enjoy the view out to sea when I needed to think. A couple of grapevines in barrels had climbed the structure and were well established, their leaves already beginning to turn as the cool of autumn approached. It had seemed a frivolous gesture at the time, to plant them, but I could never stand to be too far away from the rhythm of the vines.

From this vantage point, I could also survey the regimented fields of vines as they ran down to the headland and the sea beyond. Despite my additions, the portable office and the surrounding area, complete now with its earth moving equipment, still had the overwhelming feeling of a construction zone. Bright yellow and orange hard hats and vests hung on hooks on the wall and a set of steel-capped boots sat beside the doorway.

Years of accumulated plans, consents and council files sat in old wooden wine crates on one side of the room. Despite council's attempt to keep all of their records online, there were still a number of charts, documents, engineering reports and consents that needed to be on site in written form. I had to keep the material available for council inspectors who regularly arrived from the mainland without notice.

Another reason that I couldn't have Seb working on the project. He had a tendency to order council inspectors off our land at whim.

Nick would have been more suited to this kind of work, but he and his twin brother, Ben were both currently in Switzerland enjoying an extended period of rest and recreation. I'd seen them both not more than six months ago when we'd all enjoyed a skiing holiday at Zermatt under the shadow of The Matterhorn.

I'd practically inhaled my sandwich and feeling comfortably full, I sat back enjoying the visual feast of watching Grace eat. The moment I'd set eyes on her splayed on the floor in front of me, I'd seriously started to reconsider my swearing off of women.

There was something about the way the woman held herself. An assurance or determination that I'd not seen in quite some time. She seemed decidedly unafraid of me or the consequences of challenging my authority.

I liked that. The only woman I'd ever seen that kind of behaviour in around me was my mother.

It was a refreshing change from the pliable and willing women I'd spent the better part of the last two years with on the European circuit.

Never underestimate the independent streak in New Zealand women, I reminded myself. I'm not sure why I hadn't seen it before? Maybe I'd been to focussed on what was happening outside the confines of the antipodean islands I'd been born in.

Now, as I watched this curvaceous woman tucking into a roast beef and salad sandwich, my cock twitched, wondering what it might feel like to have those lips around its girth.

She looked over the desk at me and smiled as she wiped a smear of mayonnaise from her chin with her thumb. I couldn't be sure if it was intentional, but her eyes never left mine as she popped her thumb in her mouth and licked it clean.

My cock twitched again in response. I cleared my throat and undid the top button of my shirt. I wondered whether or not this woman had any idea of the effect she was having on me?

I turned my head to the view out to sea and attempted to direct my mind back to the job at hand, the reason I'd invited Grace here in the first place.

The project.

The project that meant so much to me and upon which hinged a large portion of my plans to reinvigorate the estate.

I ignored the protestations of my cock. It had done nothing but get me into intolerable situations lately and I'd decided that we were going on an enforced period of abstinence from women.

Still, the idea rattled around in my head—I wonder what Grace would look like lying naked in my bed?

I closed my eyes and shut out the nagging thought.

"So, you can see that we're sat amongst a development site here," I said waving my hand in the direction of the beginning of the pile of spoils that were being dug from the hillside.

"I have some photographs of the kind of space I'm trying to develop once the excavation has been completed."

I brought up the folder of photographs that I'd taken while I was away in Italy and turned my laptop around so that we could both look at the screen.

Grace wiped her luscious lips with a napkin and then pulled her chair closer to my desk. As she leaned forward, I caught the scent of her floral perfume. It reminded me of the roses that we grew at the ends of each row of vines—vivid pinks, yellows and reds brought the vineyard alive with colour in the summer. I hauled my eyes from the enticing view of her breasts back to my computer screen. Once my head cleared and I focussed on the pictures on the screen, I pointed out the various highlights of my fact finding trip to Italy.

"Where were these taken?" she asked.

"Tuscany, in Italy," I replied and I watched as she redoubled her concentration on the images. "A beautiful little hillside village called, Montepulciano. I wanted to visit the labyrinth of underground cellars first hand."

Images that I'd captured of the stairwells and cellars, with their intricate brickwork and high vaulted ceilings crossed the computer screen.

"Italy," Grace sighed, "it's one of the places that I'd love to visit when I go to Europe."

"When are you going?"

"In two months," she replied her eyes still held in rapt attention on the screen as the images of my trip to Italy continued to play.

Two months. That didn't give me much time to work with her.

"Did mother know you were leaving in two months?"

I watched as a blush crawled up Grace's face. She turned from the computer and looked across as me and then shook her head.

"No." Then she said as an afterthought, "But my contract stipulates that I only have to give two weeks' notice."

That may well be the case, I thought, but I was certain Kathryn wouldn't have recommended Grace if she knew her to be leaving. That was the real trouble with the island— transient people and transient staff.

My own family had been here for generations working the land on the Island one way or another. Even though we spent time overseas, we always returned to our Island home. There was something about this place that even I had to admit I missed when I was travelling in Europe.

"I'm planing to make Italy one of the places that I stay when I'm studying," Grace said, oblivious to the current torment in my head. If she was only going to be here for the next two months, was it really worth me taking her on now? "I'm really looking forward to being able to visit places like this." Grace said as she continued to scroll through the vast array of photographs that I had on my computer.

"They're well worth a visit," I said wondering how much work we could conceivably achieve here before she left.

"What are you going to study?" I hadn't planned on making small talk. In fact, right now all I wanted to study was the form and shape of Grace's body. Preferably in my bed.

I reminded myself that it wasn't less than half a day ago that I was swearing off women for good. But finding out that the lovely Grace would be leaving in about eight weeks brought my carnal appetites back into strict focus.

In an instant, I couldn't recall ever being this attracted to a woman I'd only just met. Grace was so different from the thin, dark women that usually blipped on my radar. But there was something about the way her body moved, the curiosity in her bright green eyes and the way her clothes hugged that voluptuous figure.

"Photography and fine arts," she said with a wistful look. "I've wanted to go to Italy all my life. The architecture and the history have fascinated me for as long as I can remember."

"Well," I said "that's just a wonderful coincidence, because I'm determined to create a little of Italy right here on the Island and I guess you're just the woman I've been looking for to help me achieve that vision."

"Really?" Grace lost the dreamy look on her face, her attention suddenly back on me.

Back on me in such a way that I knew her look was responsible for the heat that crawled up my body.

If I felt like this when she looked at me while we sat in my office, what the hell would I feel like if she were looking at me across a glass of our finest Merlot back in my wing of the house?

I tried to get my mind back on the business at hand. "So," I said clearing my throat and forcing my eyes away from the temptation of Grace's body. "You will have noticed the earth moving equipment that's arrived here in the last few days."

"Me and half of the Island," Grace said as she cast her eyes out of the small window of the portacom to the large yellow and orange machinery that stood idle in the fields beyond. "I wondered what was going on the other day when I arrived for work and had to brave my way across a picket line of protestors." She smiled, a wicked smile that did things to me that I didn't want to acknowledge. "I thought for a moment that the staff you'd fired were going to stop me coming in to work. Then I saw our local politician and the camera crew stood talking with Malcolm from Fish & Bird and I knew it had to have something to do with the environment."

"That didn't worry you?" I asked, my interest genuinely piqued. There was something about Grace's calm assurance that made me want to rile her. Maybe I was just in the habit of wanting to rile women at the moment. But Grace was going away, I reminded myself. I'd removed her from mother's restaurant and told her that she was going to work here with me. Perhaps she'd taken the attitude that she had nothing to lose.

What would I do?

Maybe fire her, but then she could always go back to working for mother. It wouldn't be the first time that Kathryn had taken back a worker that one of her sons had dismissed from a different part of the vineyard.

"Well, there's always someone on the Island doing something that Fish & Bird aren't happy with and the Pearson family," now she shrugged and her breasts pressed together in an alluring manner that made me swallow hard, "there's never a week goes by that one of you isn't in the press about something."

Usually my problematic younger brother, I was tempted to say, but I held my tongue. It was of interest to me to see how someone who worked for us saw the family.

Perhaps it wasn't such a bad idea having Grace here.

I cocked my head to one side. "You're not afraid of telling it like it is?"

She shook her head. "I've never been one to back down from a challenge if that's what you're saying."

"How long have you been on the Island?" I asked Grace.

"What's that got to do with working for you on this project?"

The speed with which she spun the question back at me took me by surprise. "Part of the job will be dealing with the locals."

"In what way?" I watched as Grace's spine stiffened. Had I touched some kind of raw nerve?

"Keeping them informed of what's happening with the project."

"You mean spinning it so that they won't continue to object and get in the way of your outrageous plans?"

I arched an eyebrow, she definitely wasn't afraid of standing up to me. I liked that. I rearranged the way I sat in my chair and then leaned forward, putting Grace on the spot. She didn't flinch or let up with eye contact for a second. I liked that even more.

"My plans may be outrageous, Ms Richards," I saw a slight movement in her body as I addressed her in this formal way, "but I can assure you that they will not need any kind of spinning."

"What will they need then?" she asked, as she leaned forward to meet the challenge of my body with her own.

Yes.

A glass of our best vintage and an evening with Ms Grace Richards was going to be on the agenda well before the week was out if I had any further say in the matter.

I cleared my throat. "They will need someone who is able to communicate at a local level with the locals." I wasn't about to let the challenge go. "Which brings me neatly back to my question. How long have you been on the Island?"

Grace leaned back in her seat and I found myself

mirroring her actions. "I've been coming here with my parents ever since I was a child." She folded the napkin that had been sitting on her knee into a tiny square, flattened it with her hands and then placed it with care on the empty plate where her lunch had resided. "I shouldn't even have to qualify myself to you, but my grandparents built the old yellow board and batten bach down at Spindle Bay back in the 1920's."

The one landholding family who had been holding out on development on the waterfront at Spindle Bay for an age. Grace's assertions didn't make any sense to me.

"But that property has been in the hands of the Levinson family for years. We've been trying to purchase it so we can complete a development and they won't sell to us." I thought about how long it had been since we'd tried to acquire a quarter acre of prime waterfront property. "Well, forever it seems." What she was saying to me didn't make sense.

Grace nodded. "My mother's maiden name is Levinson." Could that be a smug smile forming on her lips?

"And your mother wouldn't consider selling the land for what it's worth?"

"She might. But she certainly wouldn't sell it to the Pearson family."

"Why not?" I was genuinely perplexed. "From what I know you never come here. The building is vacant except over the summer season, when I guess you must rent it out to holidaymakers. Why wouldn't you and your family want to sell it and use the considerable amount of money we'd offer you?"

I couldn't be sure because I hadn't looked at the file for some time, but my last recollection was that we'd offered the family in excess of five million dollars for the quarter acre. The bach itself we would have turned into firewood. The money simply reflected the value of the dirt that the old house sat on.

Grace shrugged. "You'd have to ask my mum that question. The property's been in the family for generations now and I guess it's always been somewhere to come in the summer." A scowl crossed Grace's face. "Well, mum was happy to come here until your family started all the development around the beach. She says that the place has never quite felt the same since those huge plaster and brick mansions have been appearing on the water's edge."

"You can't stand in the way of progress."

"Well," Grace laughed, "it appears that my mother can and she has done."

There was something else that the Levinson family were standing in the way of—but for the life of me, I couldn't quite put my mind to what it might be.

Clearly, I'd been working too hard on the preliminary works for the first wine cave that I wanted to build. Excavation would begin as soon as the engineers signed off on the plans and I expected that to happen late this afternoon.

The machinery that stood idle out the front of the portacom would be kicking into action tomorrow and I wanted to make sure that Grace was on board with the project.

"Anyway," I said bringing the conversation back around to why we were here. "I didn't drag you out of the dining room to get a complete history of your family—although it has been interesting to note that you've probably spent nearly as many years on this Island as I have."

I guessed that Grace might be a little less than four or five years younger than myself, which put her at twenty-two or twenty-three. The usual age for most New Zealanders to be looking at spreading their wings and heading overseas.

My twin brothers, Ben and Nick were both into their

second year of overseas travel and it wouldn't be long before they were heading back home to take their rightful places on the estate.

The sooner we could get Seb overseas the better as far as I was concerned. He'd been making noises about going to New York on some kind of wild hospitality experience. He loved working in the kitchen, despite my mother's horror at the thought of her precious Seb hanging off the end of a frying pan.

Grace eyed me with what? Curiosity, I couldn't be sure. "I suppose we could have spent about the same amount of time here, if you take into account the years you spent on the mainland at private school."

I didn't want to be reminded about the years I'd spent incarcerated at one of Auckland's finest boarding schools. Being away from the Island had been purgatory. Followed by three years at University in Switzerland. The time away had almost cured me of any wanderlust. In fact, I think the last excursion to Italy must have killed any ideas I had about spending time outside of New Zealand.

The world, as Grace would find out soon enough, was not the fascinating and wondrous place that many youthful New Zealanders believed it to be.

I stood up and walked out onto the small deck attached to the portacom. "You'd have to go a long way anywhere in the world to beat a view like this one," I said to Grace as I cast my eye across the sparkling water of the Hauraki Gulf. There was something comforting about standing on this prime ridgeline and looking out down the military lines of the vines as they marched toward the beach below. The colour of the sun on the water as it began its lazy afternoon descent and the dark silhouette of the volcano Rangitoto with the city of Auckland sitting across the other side.

"I'll never tire of this view," I said to Grace. "You

remember the beauty of this place when you're stuck in some cupboard masquerading as an apartment in Europe. Believe me, there's something about this Island and the way it calls you home."

"Won't be calling me home," Grace said in a determined tone. "Now, what was it that you brought me over here to do?"

CHAPTER 5

*G*race
The afternoon passed in a whirlwind of trying
to keep my mind on the things that Harry was
showing me and ignoring the siren call of my body.

I didn't want to find Harry Pearson attractive.

In fact, the idea caused me all manner of grief.

As I walked back down the gravel driveway to the haven
of our little family bach, I felt the way I had always felt as I
approached the yellow board and batten home. The stress of
the day began to wash away from my body in the same way
that the sea washed up on the beach in front of the building.

The idea of another one of the Pearson monolithic buildings appearing on this site made my insides curl.

The picket fence out the front by the roadside may well
have been missing a few coats of paint, but my mother's well
established garden in the front of the house made up for that.
I passed the gnarled trunk of the Black Dorris plum tree with
its light smattering of lichen and noticed an old birds nest
tucked high in the branches. Not only had the old tree been
feeding my family all of my life, but it was also home to a

number of the tiny wax eyes in the area. The tree produced far more fruit than we were ever able to consume. As a child, I'd taken my first faltering steps into the commercial world, selling bags of fallen plums over Christmas from the front gate to the tourists who poured onto the island.

I should have known back then that commerce wasn't my calling.

In those days, tourists only came during the Christmas summer holiday period, now there seemed to be a continual stream of them up and down the road from the ferry building.

When had it gotten so busy?

I looked at the surrounding street area with new eyes. Suburbia encroached on what had been a sleepy island road. When we first came here, the road wasn't even tar sealed. On a hot summer's day, the leaves of the feijoa trees that stood between the picket fence and the boundary proper would be covered in a fine layer of dust. I was always grateful that the large, sweet green fruit didn't ripen until autumn when the crowds had left and the rains had come again to wash away the choking dust.

I could remember standing under those old feijoa trees eating so many fruits that I came out in hives. Who shook the trees and collected the fruit now that we didn't visit often, I wondered? Maybe no-one other than the local bird life by the look of the carpet of blackened and rotted fruit that sat beneath the canopy of the silver green leaves.

I stopped in the middle of the driveway and took a moment to really look around me. The discussions I'd had with Harry this afternoon made me take stock of my thoughts around the old bach.

In my haste to look forward to where I wanted to be—maybe I'd been too quick to turn my back on what had been a huge part of my upbringing.

Mum's prize roses were hidden from the salt-laden spray that battered the front of the house and continued to bloom, despite the lack of her critical care. Large old fashioned cabbage roses in shades of pink, lilac and white could be found meandering their way around the winding shell paths that littered the expansive grounds.

Spring was well gone and the traditional cottage garden that had been regenerating itself for decades had survived another dry summer. No doubt due, in part, to the protection from the small stand of macrocarpa trees that had been part of the original shelter belt when the land was farmed many years ago.

I looked at the angular shapes of the tall old trees. "Your days would be numbered," I said to them. If Harry Pearson got a hold of the land, those magnificent trees would be the first things to go to make way for more housing.

A light nip in the early evening breeze made me shiver. Or was it the thought of what someone like Harry Pearson or his brothers would do to a beautiful property like this if they got their hands on it?

I turned the key in the well worn lock and opened the front door.

The familiar scent of a lifetime of memories met me as I crossed the threshold of my home.

This tiny building had originally been two rooms with a fireplace in the centre when my grandfather built it back in the 1920's. I didn't need mum to tell me ever again that my grandfather had worked for a car importer. The vehicles came by steamer from England in wooden crates. The wood that had carried the cars over the Atlantic and then Pacific Ocean were collected with care by my grandfather and used to line the walls of this building.

I'll never forget when I was nine years old and we began to make some extensions to the property, my delight at reading the writing on the old car crates as they came into view.

Somewhere inside those walls, my older brother and sister and me had written our names and drawn around our hand prints. We were as much a part of the building as the generations who'd enjoyed it before us. As happens in families like ours, now I was the only person who came and visited.

Mum couldn't stand to come since the apartment block went in at the south end of the beach. My brother, Cory was in the navy and never in New Zealand it seemed any more and my sister, Beverley had married an eminent barrister and they had their own bach now down at Lake Taupo. She said that she loved their house on the lake more than the bach at the Island because it was modern. We were still living somewhere between the late 1960's and the early 1970's here. But that didn't bother me the way that it bothered my siblings. Compared to some of the crummy flats I'd been living in Auckland—this place was warm and light and comfortable.

I opened the French doors that let in the view of the beachfront and allowed the fresh sea air to permeate the small living and kitchen space.

I picked up my camera—it was never too far from my hand when I wasn't working.

Dog walkers were out in force on the sand walking their four just sorry-footed companions and I waved to a couple of regulars out with their ambling golden retriever. The shaggy dog lay in the water's edge, no doubt cooling off after running the length of the beach and I couldn't help but take a few shots of the damp dog as he frolicked along ahead of his owners.

I liked it here—despite the fact that I knew I had to move on in a couple of months. I had friends here and in the short time that I'd been living full time in the community, I'd made myself indispensable to Forest & Bird. I was helping them to catalogue the bird life that lived along the shoreline and photographing the great progress that was being made with the native plantings in the borderline splash zones.

I left my camera on the outside table and pulled a half empty bottle of wine out of the fridge in the kitchen. I decided I'd have a glass of wine and wait for the sun to begin its ritual of sliding below the horizon. The light at this time of the year set the sky off in spectacular colour and I wanted to try to capture some of the magic.

I found myself one of the many mis-matching wine glasses from behind the blue and white curtain that had hung across the crockery shelf for as long as I could remember. I didn't know whether or not the material happened to be of industrial grade, or more likely, knowing my family, mum had managed to secure an old bolt of the material on the cheap and simply replaced the curtain every few years or so as it began to disintegrate.

I poured myself a glass of wine and ran my fingers over the Pearson's gold embossed label. I really didn't need the complication of working with Harry Pearson at this time in my life.

Why hadn't I just said no when Kathryn Pearson said I should go and work with him? I took a sip of the wine and closed my eyes, the flavour of the grapes tickling my taste-buds. I always felt that I could taste the salt that collected on the grapes in the wine itself, along with notes of citrus.

I took a deep, soothing breath and sat myself down on the couch in front of the French doors. From here, I could see out to the beach, watch the comings and goings of everyone, but not feel as if I was out on display for all the world to see. I enjoyed my privacy—but that would be something surely lacking from this piece of land if it were sold and redeveloped like the neighbouring properties.

I probably wasn't the best person for Harry Pearson to be employing to help manage a large extension of the vineyard.

He talked about bringing a little of Italy here, but what about retaining the nature of the Island? Wasn't that the reason so many people came here? Granted, their wine business had brought employment to the area and people needed to work, but there was something about some of Harry's grandiose plans that didn't sit well with me.

Harry

It was dark by the time I locked the door of the portacom and headed back to my wing of the house.

The sun had set across the gulf, but in some parts twilight had not quite yet seeped from the sky. I could plainly see where the last of the blue hue of the sky had been absorbed by the dark night. A band of colour skirted the top of Rangitoto making the volcano look as if it had been outlined with a pink marker pen. The Sky Tower resembled some kind of strange, magical wand sitting amidst the multiple lights of the city of Auckland and an explosion of sparkling stars.

I made the decision to leave my quad bike and walk the almost two kilometres back to my apartment in the house. I'd missed my morning swim and I needed the exercise.

I'd been visiting a gym while I was in Europe and I was aware that I'd let my fitness regime go since I'd been back on the vineyard. The early autumn evening was still warm, but I could feel the beginning of the cool nights approaching which I knew would begin the annual process of turning the leaves on the vines the beautiful shades of red and gold that I so loved.

As I walked the headland path, all I could hear was the

distant sound of the waves washing across the pebbles on the beach below. The odd hoot from a local owl pierced the rhythmic wash of the ocean and I could hear the call of native Kiwi that lived deep in the bush. The sound of a girl's laughter from the back of the vineyard's kitchen drifted to me on the light breeze. No doubt the last of the waiting staff or the kitchen staff cleaning up after another long day.

Kathryn refused to keep the vineyard kitchen open later than 7pm, so the last diners were on their way well before the last ferry left the island.

I meandered along the dark tracks. I could easily have navigated them with my eyes closed—I'd walked them so many times in the past.

I skirted the formal gardens on my way into my wing of the house. The entire property had been built based on the design of an English stately home. A large rectangular building to accommodate my parents and any guests that they may care to have stay with them and then, running off from the main building, individual wings for each of their four sons.

Each wing had enough separate accommodation for a small family and I could ostensibly live in my wing of the house and never speak to my parents, or my siblings.

That, however, rarely happened as most of us chose to have a family breakfast in the room that mother had aptly named, "The Great Hall".

Tonight the main wing of the house remained quiet, the only lights coming from the wing where my youngest brother Seb resided.

No doubt, he'd have another one of the string of women in there with him who seemed to rotate on a regular basis. I couldn't complain. I'd had my own share of women through my apartment over the years. I'd promised myself that wouldn't be happening again now I was back from Europe—

but I couldn't seem to shake the enticing image of Grace from my mind.

The way the sunlight had caught her hair this afternoon on our walk down to my office. The endearing way she had twirled a piece of her hair between her fingers while I showed her files and helped her become familiar with what I'd loosely called a filing system. She was at pains to explain to me that dropped pieces of paper into old wine boxes could not be construed as an appropriate way to keep my records in order.

My stomach growled and I was reminded that I hadn't had anything to eat since Grace had sat opposite me this afternoon. A quick trip to the main house and I found myself face-to-face with Kathryn who sat at the head of the large table in the Great Hall.

"Ah, Harry," she patted the top of the table, a clear indication that I should set aside the demands of my stomach and bow to those of the Matriarch of the family.

"Yes, Mother." I greeted her with a peck on the cheek and pulled out one of the large, cattle skin covered chairs that lined the long table.

The Great Hall could comfortably accommodate seating for eighteen people at the dining table. Three sides of the room were floor-to-ceiling glass, which afforded the room an almost three hundred and sixty degree view out across the headland and out to the gulf beyond.

In the dark of the evening and with the lights dimmed the way mother preferred to have them at this time of the night, the windows took on a sheen of black. The fourth wall housed the kitchen proper. A modern kitchen had been installed inside of what looked like an old fashioned Victorian hearth.

The granite bench top that sat in front of the hearth acted as a breakfast bar if only a couple of members of the family were passing through. Mother, of course, preferred at all times to seat herself at the large table—even if eating by herself—which she seemed to be doing more and more often lately.

"Did Seb not join you tonight?" I asked.

The scent of the fish pie that mother had brought from the restaurant set my stomach growling again.

Mother arched an eyebrow. "No he didn't. He spent the evening in the bistro with a young lady who struggled to understand a word of English. But you go and find yourself a plate." She paused and then added with a wry smile, "From the sound of things, you've barely eaten all day."

I pulled a plate from the cupboard. "I don't think intelligent conversation is what Seb's looking for at the moment."

Mother waved her hand. "He's young. So he's sowing a few wild oats."

Nothing fazed my mother. But then, having lived with my father for so long, why would I expect anything less?

She served me a large portion of the pie and then pushed a fresh green salad toward me. "Get some greens."

"I'm not seventeen any more," I reminded her.

"None of you have been teenagers for quite a few years now," she said with what may have been a wistful look in her eye.

"You didn't call me here to discuss the fact that we were all grown men," I said as I allowed a forkful of chef's latest cooking endeavour to melt in my mouth. "How does he make it taste so good?"

"You get the best when you pay good money," Mother replied as she tossed another portion of salad greens on my plate.

"How about you have a glass of wine with your mother now that you're here?"

"Red or white?" I asked.

Mother laughed, the happy sound filled the room and made me smile. "After the exorbitant amount we spent on sending you to Europe, I can't believe you're actually asking me that question. What's on your plate?"

"This is home," I replied, "not the restaurant. No-one's going to report you to the culinary police just because you decide to have red with white meat.

"There's a nice pinot in the fridge."

I collected the wine and two cut-glass crystal glasses and poured me and mother a drink.

She held her glass aloft and the high-pitched sound of the two touching each other echoed off the hard surfaces that surrounded us.

"To your new venture," she said.

I nodded in acknowledgment. I'd never been sure whether or not mother had approved of my plans for the vineyard, but in any event, she'd given me my head and allowed me to continue in the face of opposition from the local community. Not that opposition from the local community had ever prevented a Pearson from doing anything in the past.

"How do you think Grace will be?" Mother asked as she put her glass down on the table.

"She's leaving in two months."

"Really?"

I continued to eat, pushing the salad greens around the plate despite the occasional disapproving glance from mother.

"Yes. She was at pains this afternoon to advise me that she was under no obligation to provide us with notice until two weeks prior to her scheduled departure."

"She's quite right," mother sniffed. "At least eat your olives, dear."

I speared the green, rolling fruit with their peculiar tang

and tried not to feel like a twelve-year-old being chastised for not clearing his plate.

"Send Grace back to the restaurant tomorrow and I'll find you someone else."

"No," I shook my head and then took a sip of the refreshing pinot, "I'll work with Grace. The project's interesting enough that she might just decide to put off her travel plans."

Mother eyed me over her own wine glass. "Okay, but the offer stands. You can send her back any time." Mother's eyes widened, "Or maybe you might have a little more than a passing professional interest in the young lady."

"You know I don't mix business with my personal life."

"Of course," mother replied, taking a sip of the pinot and following up with a wide smile. I think I may well have heard for the first time in my life a hint of disbelief in my mother's tone. "You might like to think about bringing her along to the end of harvest banquet."

I raised my eyebrows, "Did you not hear me say that I don't mix business with pleasure."

"I'm thinking about the business," mother said.

"How?"

"If you want to keep on side with the locals, then I can't think of a better time to introduce Grace to those in the know."

"I'll think about it."

As always mother had a valid point and I wasn't quite sure who I was trying to convince that I didn't mix business and pleasure.

race

It had been nearly a week now since I'd agreed to take on the job with Harry. Aside from the odd excursion out to speak with the locals, I'd spent most of my time with him holed up inside this portacom.

Harry, I'd discovered, wasn't as terrifying as I originally thought him to be. He'd been considerate and taken his time letting me get to grips with the project.

Having spent this much time alone with the man, I'd come to understand a little of the driven nature of the Pearson male who had employed me.

Harry, it turned out was a man with a vast vision for the Pearson vineyard and the Island beyond. He spent time at length explaining to me how he planned to bring to our Island a little of the country where he'd been residing for the last months.

Harry commanded respect—the same as his mother, Kathryn. In fact, Harry didn't just command it, he demanded it from everyone around him. I'd spent plenty of time laughing and joking with the construction crews who worked around the hillside, burrowing into the earth like ants. They seemed so out of place in the autumnal green of the surrounding fields in their bright orange and yellow high visibility vests.

As soon as Harry arrived the jovial atmosphere changed. The workmen put their collective heads down and scurried off—it was the same way with most of the staff in the restaurant. In fact, all Harry had to do was walk into a room and he had the full attention of everyone.

He didn't have to say a word.

It was something that I'd watched his mother, Kathryn do and secretly, I wondered who had taught who how to dominate in this way. The Pearson family were a formidable team, but now that I'd spent some time with Harry, I began to wonder who in fact held the reins of control within the family.

As I watched the construction crew return to their work, I couldn't help but notice that a number of the lines of vines down the hillside had started to change, taking on a hue of light gold as the leaves began to turn prior to their final fall in winter. The landscape took on a beautiful, golden glow after the harvest. The vines became somewhat bedraggled and wild and, for some strange reason it was only now that I was beginning to realise how much I loved them for that.

"Grace," the sound of Harry's voice cut through my thoughts. "Can I see you in here please?" Always so polite. The use of the word 'please' conveyed a degree of civility but the word was, in fact, redundant. Harry wasn't asking me to do anything—he was demanding with a pretence of politeness.

I swallowed and returned to the intensity of the shared portacom space. I had no idea whether or not Harry felt the tension that pulsated through the area when we were alone— but I certainly did.

I tried to ignore the mounting sexual energy that was building between us, convincing myself that it was all in my imagination. But the second Harry called my name, my body became hyper-aware of him.

"Yes?" I tried to sound casual and professional. A difficult thing to pull off when every atom in my body screamed at me to lick this man's face. I wondered, not for the first time, whether I should ask to be returned to the restaurant. I liked to think that I was a simple girl from Auckland, who could mind her own business, get ready to head off overseas and keep my libido in check in the meantime. It wasn't as if I'd had a lot of experience around men like Harry Pearson. In fact, I'd had none. If he was the kind of man that I was going to find in Europe, then, quite frankly, I was in real trouble.

I stood in front of Harry, trying not to notice the cut of his jaw, the way his throat moved when he swallowed the coffee that he held in his hand.

"I brought you a flat white, just the way you like it." He held his hand out to me, a cup of coffee in a takeaway cup with the Vineyard's logo on the side.

My mouth watered. I couldn't be sure if it was because of the scent of coffee in the air or the presence of Harry.

I took the hot container from his hand and our fingers brushed together. A shot of electricity ran up my arm. Clearly, I was working far too hard. Or I'd drunk one glass too many of wine last night.

"Thank you," I said as I cradled the small paper cup, with its white plastic lid to my breast.

Harry's eyes never left mine.

Silence hung in the air between us.

Had he felt the same thing at the touch of our hands?

Surely not.

Get a grip. I said to myself, *he's a billionaire vintner who comes from a prestigious family—he's never going to look at a girl like you.*

The fact I'd had no experience with a man of Harry Pearson's calibre weighed heavy on my mind.

He was probably just being nice, bringing me a coffee, I reassured myself. It didn't have to mean something.

The honest truth was that my relationship with men had been pretty fraught. Yes, I'd had a boyfriend for a while at university, but things hadn't exactly gone well. I still couldn't be too sure that part of the reason I was heading to Europe was so that I could get away from the heinous memories. It felt as if everywhere I looked in Auckland I could find a reason to think about Nathan.

Had it really been that much of a relationship? Most of the time we'd gone out, he'd get drunk and we'd end up in bed.

Honestly, I couldn't see what all the fuss was about sex.

Yet a simple touch of Harry's hand had reverberated around my body.

Sex with Nathan had left me feeling cold, dirty and somewhat alone. It certainly hadn't been the most important part of the so-called relationship that we'd been engaged in for almost a year.

In the end, we agreed to go our separate ways. He'd landed a job as junior counsel at a barrister's chambers and had high ideas about his position in law. The relationship had been fizzling out for months before we made that final break, but my spectacular failure in commerce had been the last straw.

I thought I'd been ready for it to all come to an end, but looking back now, if I was honest, the break from Nathan had driven me back to Hauraki Island. Here, in a familiar landscape I could lick my wounds of embarrassment and make plans to leave the country for good.

It seemed silly now. Abandoning everything and everyone I knew because of a failed relationship. The longer I'd been on the Island, the more I'd come to see that commerce and me were never going to be great together.

A simple touch from Harry had spun my head to so many strange places. Being around him had been like waking up from a long winter sleep.

I could feel the sexual side of my being yawning and stretching. That part of me that I'd shut down while I was with Nathan had crawled out of her winter hibernation and opened her eyes.

"You seem to be getting along well with the contractors," Harry said eventually breaking the strange silence. He took another sip of his coffee and I had the urge to run my hand along the swell of his neck as the liquid went down his throat.

I cleared my own throat. "My understanding is that part of my role is to smooth things out between the contractors and the locals." Was he jealous? A tiny part of me wanted him to be jealous.

A knock at the door prevented Harry from responding. The head contractor poked his head through the door. "Hey, we're done here for the day," he said.

Harry looked at his watch. I wondered how much that watch was worth? I knew its understated elegance. Everything about Harry spoke of understated elegance.

"It's only 4pm. You've at least another three hours of daylight."

"Knock off is 4pm," he replied. "We're under strict instructions from Grace here," he tipped his head in my direction, together with a beaming smile, "to make sure that we don't go a minute over and annoy the residents."

"Is that right?" Harry turned dark blue eyes on me—eyes

that mirrored the colour of the sea that surrounded the Island.

"The job description," I replied trying to stay calm under his intense scrutiny, "keeping the locals happy. This is part of the plan."

"But what about this plan?" Harry said as he swept his hand in the direction of the raft of complex drawings that were pinned across the entire wall on the far side of the portacom.

I looked to the door again and the head contractor had left.

Coward, I thought.

I'd been so engrossed in my work that I hadn't realised it was so late in the day. Without the familiar rotations of diners coming and going, I seemed to lose hours here in Harry's domain.

"They're making good progress, right?" I tried to reassure my demanding boss.

Harry begrudgingly gave me a nod. It was only then that I realised he stood in front of me in a pair of jeans and a light green t-shirt that seemed to hug the muscles of his chest in all the right places.

I took a sip of the coffee—the buzz of the caffeine reminded me that I'd not eaten enough today. Working this far away from the restaurant and without the enticing scent of food preparation meant that my appetite seemed to have vanished. Or maybe it was working so close to Harry. My body was in a state of constant arousal around him. I couldn't even blame it on the change of work—or that fact that some days I felt as if I didn't know what I was doing. All I had to do was be at Harry's beck and call. The job wasn't so hard. What seemed difficult was burying my mounting feelings around Harry.

"I guess if that's what it's going to take to keep the locals at bay, I may have to bend to your desires," he said his voice washing over me and making my skin tingle.

How did he make the word desire sound so dirty? A tiny voice in my brain asked.

"I'm glad you can see things from my point-of-view." I couldn't help tilting my head to the side and giving him one of my most alluring smiles. There was something about being around him that seemed to have awoken my ovaries from their period of enforced abstinence. The sex siren who had awoken from her long sleep seemed to be firmly in control.

"Forget the coffee," Harry said putting his cup aside and digging around in a wine crate that sat behind his desk. "We're celebrating your first week on the job."

He pulled out a bottle of the vineyard's fine cabernet sauvignon. Then he dug around in another box and found two glasses. He polished them, the same way I'd seen the wine waiters in the restaurant polish the glasses before they poured a wine. It wasn't something that I expected to see from Harry. The simple gesture brought home the fact that, aside from his surname and the millions of dollars that I knew this vineyard generated for him and his family, essentially he was just another man who lived on the island.

By the time he'd finished, both of the glasses sparkled.

"Come on, out here," Harry said as he directed me to the small verandah attached to the front of the porticom.

"Sit down," I did as I was told. I'd come to the conclusion that I was pretty powerless in the presence of this man. Besides, he was paying my wages. If he wanted me to slack off on his time, then who was I to argue?

Harry poured a glass of wine and handed it to me. The afternoon sunlight danced through the rose-coloured liquid. The sweet aroma of the wine made my mouth water, or again was that the proximity of Harry—I could never be sure.

"Cheers," he said as he put the bottle down on the small table that sat between our chairs and then held his glass aloft. I touched mine to his and the sound drifted down the valley and out toward the expanse of the Hauraki Gulf.

"Did you manage to speak to the woman from the Island News?"

"Yes," I said. Ever since the earth movers had arrived on the Island there had been increasing interest in what the Pearson family were doing now. "She said that she'll draft an article and I've managed to persuade her to send it to us for checking before she runs it."

Harry nodded his approval. "The power of the advertising dollar."

"What do you mean?"

"We spend thousands a month with them. They're not going to run a story that we don't approve."

I turned to face him. "You mean you've basically bought the press?" The idea appalled me.

"Not at all," he replied. "They're free to print whatever they want."

Yes, I thought, probably about as free as I am to decide that I didn't want to work here with Harry.

Suddenly the wine didn't taste so sweet and
the view didn't look quite so appealing.

I got up out of my chair, "Look, if you don't need me here working, I should get on home."

Harry stood up, effectively blocking my retreat to collect my things from the office.

"Have I said something to offend you?"

He stood so close to me our wine glasses were nearly touching.

The bulk of the man overwhelmed me.

My mouth went dry.

My heart began to beat a staccato march and I took a steadying gulp of the wine in an attempt to calm myself.

All that did was increase the heat that seemed to radiate from my body.

"No!" I said a little too loud.

Harry unsettled me further by stepping aside and letting me pass. He followed me back into the office, casually seating himself on the edge of his desk while he watched me gather my things.

My hands were shaking. I tried to convince myself it was the cumulative effect of the coffee, the wine and lack of food.

Harry had nothing to do with the way I was feeling.

Who are you trying to kid? That tiny, annoying voice in my brain yelled.

"Before you leave," Harry drawled in a voice that seemed to quell some of the fear and agitation I was experiencing, "I'd like you to take a look at some of the preliminary drawings I've had done for the estate."

"Sure," I replied trying to keep the nervous squeak out of my voice. I put my bag back down on the chair. Part of my brain screamed at me to just go—but my ovaries seemed to be in control of the situation.

Harry pulled a roll of large drawings from the same corner of the room where the wine had been hiding.

I watched the muscles on his back flex under his shirt as he rolled the papers out on his desk. I couldn't tear my eyes away from the area where his green t-shirt met at the back of his blue jeans. As he stretched across the desk, the t-shirt pulled out of the jeans, exposing a strip of flesh.

Ink! Blue and red ink snaked across the base of his back.

This time, without a doubt, my mouth went dry.

I wanted to trace that ink with my fingers—see where it

went. Find out how much of Harry's body was covered by the colour.

He turned around and I felt the heat of a blush crawl up my face.

Could he read my mind? Did he know what he was doing to me?

I was so out of my depth. I should have picked up my bag and run. Instead, I took the offered glass of wine again and moved closer to Harry and the plans spread across his desk.

CHAPTER 7

*H*arry
     I knew that Grace was trying to find a way to avoid my attention and run from me.

She thought I hadn't felt the bolt of electricity that had moved between us—or maybe she thought that I hadn't noticed the way the air between us seemed to sing when we worked together.

I enjoyed having Grace around and I wasn't about to let her escape from me now.

Grace edged closer to me as I showed her the plans on my desk, close enough that I could easily have reached out and run my hands across the curve of her arse. But that wasn't my style.

I wasn't crass or crude and I certainly wasn't about to start touching a woman who was ostensibly still working for me.

"You said that you wanted to visit Italy," I said to Grace, "the first day that you were here with me.

I watched the soft curls bounce around Grace's face as

she nodded confirming that my recollection was correct. I clenched my hand into a fist, resisting the prickle of desire to stroke those soft strands of hair away from her face.

"These plans were drawn up by a draughtsman in Italy. The plan is based on an estate I visited there," I said, as I turned my attention back to the plans on my desk and away from the allure of Grace's body.

But I couldn't look away for long. I watched as a moment of confusion crossed Grace's face. "But you're working on the wine caves." She put her glass of wine down and lifted up one of the sheets of paper and then another, scrutinising the drawings. "These plans look like plans for some kind of building." She flicked through some more of the papers. I could tell by the way she was running her fingers across the paper, she found the drawings as fascinating as I found watching her look at them. "These seem to be plans for something akin to a small village," she said picking up her glass and taking a sip of the wine before her eyes connected again with mine.

I couldn't help but smile. "They are plans for a small village. I want to create a replica piazza right here on the Island."

Grace's eyes widened. "Really?"

"You like the sound of that?"

"Well," she thought about it a little. "It's not really in keeping with the Island and the surrounding area."

"We own the surrounding area. It's in keeping with our plans for what we want to do with the vineyard. Don't you think that it would be a good draw card? Bring more tourists to the Island. Stimulate the local economy?"

Grace eyed me suspiciously. "Maybe some people around here don't want more tourists on the Island. It gets busy enough as it is during the summer months."

The firm line of Grace's mouth told me that I might have hit a nerve here.

I tipped my head to one side. Took a sip of my wine and settled myself on the edge of my large desk. "But you're planning to go over to Italy as part of your travels in Europe. Why would you care what was happening back here on the Island if you've made up your mind to head over there?"

"The Island's been a part of my life for years."

"Mine too."

"Yet you want to change it." I loved the way Grace wasn't afraid to stand up to me.

"It's called progress. Don't you like progress?"

"I'm not averse to progress." She tipped her nose up into the air. Something she did when she argued with me.

"Well then you'd support a development like this?" I ran my hand across the papers that Grace had only recently been touching—I wondered what it might feel like to run my hands across Grace's bare flesh.

I took another mouthful of wine. In fact, it wasn't just my fingers that I wanted to run across Grace's bare flesh. I began to wonder what she might taste like.

How she would smell as her body responded to mine?

What kind of scent we'd make together.

The hard line in Grace's lips softened and I watched as she arched her neck and stared straight into my eyes. A look that spoke to me. It promised something sinful. I couldn't help but react.

My cock stiffened. How I would love to slide it between the line of those soft, full lips.

But not yet.

It was too soon.

Too soon after my horrific experience in Italy? Who was I kidding? More like it was too soon to be fucking my PA. We were celebrating her being on the job with me for a week. How would that look with anyone around here? Especially the people that Grace was supposed to be appeasing.

I took a step back.

Took a deep breath.

Put some space between the two of us and wrestled my treasonous body under control.

"You haven't answered my question," I reminded Grace.

"What was it again?"

She looked as lost in the energy that swirled around the two of us as me.

Fuck! I couldn't remember.

I hadn't lost myself in a woman like this. Not ever.

Control.

I was all about control and Grace seemed to be beating a path straight through my brain to my bedroom.

A tiny voice. The tiny sensible voice that seemed to have gone on holiday since I'd met Grace piped up in my head. We'd been talking about my plans for development of the vineyard.

"Why would you be opposed to bringing more visitors to the Island?"

She shrugged. "I guess it's the reason that my parents don't come to the bach anymore. It's so crowded in summer. They used to come here to escape the city and now it seems that as the city's grown, more and more people are coming here."

I still didn't understand.

"So how's that not a good thing?"

Grace swirled the balance of her wine around the glass. I'd always loved the way the liquid seemed to take its time to ease itself down the inside of the glass.

Everything about the entire process of winemaking had always intrigued me—almost as much as Grace intrigued me.

She took another sip of her wine and then looked at me. There it was again. The connection that seemed to swirl around us, the same way the wine had swirled inside the glass Grace held in her hand.

"If you're running a business," Grace replied, "or building a business the way that you're building a business," her hand drifted in the direction of the plans on my desk, "then I guess it is a good thing."

"So you won't be averse to helping me while you're here then?"

"You didn't let me finish," Grace said swallowing the balance of the wine and placing the glass with care down on my desk next to the plans.

I went to add more to her glass, but she put her hand across the top, preventing me from pouring her any more.

I cocked my head to one side.

"I need to keep my head around you." Attraction crackled in the air between us. "The combination of coffee and wine's making me giddy."

"My apologies," I said as I put the cork back in the top of the bottle.

"No need to apologise," Grace said. "But you've plainly made it clear that we're finished for the day," she made to collect her things and head for the door.

I didn't want to let her go, not quite yet.

It had only been a week and I couldn't stand the thought of being away from Grace for the coming weekend.

"Before you go," I said. She stopped at the door, turned to face me and the late afternoon sunlight caught in her hair. I had to sit on my hands the urge to reach out and touch the golden strands was so intense.

"Yes?"

"We're having a function here tomorrow night. We do it

each year. To celebrate the end of the harvest and I'd like you to attend."

I didn't know quite what had come over me. Having told my mother not less than a week ago that I wouldn't be inviting anyone to the function—here I found myself doing the one thing I said I would not do.

Grace eyed me with suspicion—the swirling attraction continued to crackle in the air. "Are you asking me, or telling me I have to be there?"

"Telling you to be there." I couldn't risk her turning me down.

"I don't recall working outside of nine to five being part of my job description."

"I'm happy to pay you double-time." Who cared if I had to bribe her to be there. Money had never been an issue for me.

"What if I have plans?"

"Cancel them."

I saw the fleeting indecision cross her face. She opened her mouth to say something and then closed it.

"You'll pay me double?"

I nodded, "Yes." I couldn't help adding, "You'll have a good time as well. I'll make sure of it."

G **race**

Clearly, I needed my head read.

Why I had just agreed to go to the end of harvest party with the most attractive man on the Island I couldn't imagine.

"A penny for them?"

"What?"

Chloe arrived at my side and fell into step with me.

"You've finished early," I replied. The faint scent of the vineyard kitchen hung on Chloe's clothes.

"Not really," she replied. "I should have finished after the lunch rush, but Chef asked me to stay on and help prepare for this evening. I've done about two hours overtime."

"Jasmine finished school nearly two hours ago, who's looking after her?" I asked.

"Mum's taken her for the night. I was thinking about getting on the ferry and having a night on the town. Want to join me?"

I'd had a few nights on the town with Chloe before—one of them I was sure had been the reason that she'd ended up being a solo mother of Jasmine.

I knew Chloe wouldn't give up Jasmine for anyone or anything, but I also knew how hard she worked to keep them both and what a struggle the last six years had been for her.

Teenage pregnancy had taken its toll on Chloe, but she'd managed to get herself a hospitality certificate and her parents helped her out as much as they could.

For almost as long as I could remember, the Waters family had owned a small home up the hill from ours. I'd spent endlessly long summers hanging out with Chloe who was two years older than me—but the age gap had never been an issue. The moment we met, we had become firm friends. We spent many summers together, at the beach and in the sleep out that had since been renovated into a home for her and Jasmine.

"I don't know," and I truly didn't. My mind kept wandering to the thought of attending the harvest festival with Harry tomorrow night. If all things were equal in the world, I would be serving the family as part of the waiting staff, not sitting beside Harry and being served by my former colleagues.

We stopped at the familiar fence line that marked the beginning of what was once the large two acre piece of land that belonged to the Waters family.

Over the years, they'd sub-divided more and more of the land and sold it to wealthy Aucklanders looking to escape the city. The original home and the renovated sleep out now sat on a little under quarter of an acre. Much like our own beachfront bach, the Waters home seemed to have missed the call of the 21st century. There was something about the quaint way the pale green weatherboard house, with its white verandah and pebble drive sat in amongst its more modern neighbours.

"Mummy!" Jasmine ran down the driveway and threw herself into Chloe's arms. With her dark curly hair, olive skin and deep brown eyes, Jasmine looked like Chloe's mini-me. As I watched mother and daughter embrace, there was no disputing Chloe was Jasmine's mother.

"How was school?" Chloe asked.

"Good," Jasmine breathed, "Mrs Henderson let me clean out Bert and Ernie all by myself and she said if you let me I can bring them home for the holidays to look after them."

Chloe rolled her eyes at me above her daughter's head. "Well, we might have to talk to Grandma about that," she explained with patience to her excited daughter, "because we'd have to make sure that Samson didn't get hold of them."

"They could be friends," Jasmine said with a hopeful look on her face.

"Dogs and rabbits aren't usually friends," Chloe said, "and we wouldn't want anything to happen to Bert and Ernie now would we?"

"No," Jasmine agreed with a shake of her head. The curls that hung in ringlets around her face swung from side-to-side. "I'll go and talk to Grandma." She went to run back to the house, but before she'd got more than a couple of steps away from us Chloe yelled, "You haven't said hello to Grace."

The little girl spun on her heels and threw herself into my stomach with a force that nearly winded me.

"Hi, Aunty Grace." Big brown eyes looked up at me from above a wide Polynesian nose. It was the only hint that her father had been of Maori descent.

Sam, although no more than a teenager himself, had tried to do the right thing by his small family. He'd moved to the Island and taken a job as a kitchen hand in the restaurant. But a fishing trip gone wrong one weekend and a lack of an adequate lifejacket meant that his body now lay in his family burial site under the gaze of Mt Taranaki.

The loss had nearly broken Chloe. She'd never looked at another man since and had devoted herself to bringing up their beautiful daughter.

We both watched the young child run back up the driveway and then disappear inside the house.

"Rabbits?" I looked at Chloe and tried to suppress a smirk.

"I know, but she's been obsessed with anything small and furry for months. I thought the chickens might be enough, but it appears not."

"At least you still get fresh eggs every morning."

An evil grin flashed across Chloe's face. "I'll invite you for Sunday roast when the rabbits come."

"Don't you dare!" The idea of eating bunny didn't sit well with me.

"So you'll come out with me tonight?"

"I don't know." I thought about Harry again. "You've got the harvest festival tomorrow, you can't have a late night."

"We'll be on the ten o'clock ferry home."

I hadn't had a night out since I couldn't remember when. The prospect of two out in a row.

"What the hell," I said with a wave of my hand. "What time should I meet you at the ferry?"

"That's my girl," Chloe said. "Besides, I deserve a night out before I have to deal with the Pearson family's Harvest Festival." She screwed up her face. "It's all right for you, now that you've landed that cushy job with Harry you won't have to spend the night serving them all."

"Yeah," I said, taking a deep breath. At least we'd have something to talk about tonight.

CHAPTER 8

G race

"What the hell do you mean, you're going to the Harvest Festival with Harry Pearson?"

"You heard me," I said as I watched the familiar ferry terminal fade into the distance behind the wash from the twin-hulled ferry.

It would be less than forty minutes until we docked at the wharf at downtown Auckland. I still couldn't believe that Chloe had so easily talked me into a night on the town.

"Where shall we go?" I asked her, "I'm not keen to spend a lot. Isn't there a new noodle house on the waterfront that's supposed to be reasonable?"

"Don't try to change the subject," Chloe said.

I didn't need to look at her to know that her eyes were drilling into me, I could feel the intensity of her stare from where I was sitting.

"Spill. What's been going on between you and Harry Pearson?"

"Nothing!"

"But you might want something to be happening," she said in a sing-song voice that I recognised from our long summers on the beach. Chloe's response confirmed that I may well have spat the word out with too much enthusiasm.

Now I did turn around and look at her.

She carried on lecturing me, complete with wagging finger.

"You know the Pearson family, right? Those boys eat women like you and me for breakfast and are on to another by the afternoon."

Seb certainly fell into that mould, but I couldn't be quite so sure about Harry. He'd been away for such a long time. Maybe he was simply more discreet than his younger brother. But I wasn't going to share that information with Chloe—well not quite yet, anyway.

"I'm going overseas in two months," I said trying to sound nonchalant.

"And you're planning to have some fun with Harry before you go?"

I readjusted myself in the plastic bucket seat. We'd slipped well past the Island headland by now and were out in the gulf proper. The end of the working week saw a slew of Aucklanders abandoning their lives in the suburbs and heading out into the gulf.

The city known as the City of Sails lived up to its name on a Friday night as many of the yacht owners climbed aboard their boats and made for the aquatic playground offered by the gulf.

Multiple inlets and islands scattered around the gulf meant that there was always somewhere for an aquatic adventurer to throw an anchor no matter which way the predominant westerly wind blew.

I concentrated on the parade of sails bobbing across the

ferry's wake and tried not to think about the prospect of some kind of fleeting affair with Harry Pearson.

Every time the man crossed my mind, my traitorous body had some kind of hormonal reaction.

"I don't need to get attached to anyone if I'm leaving." Casual affairs had never been my thing and I was determined to get overseas so I could experience the world.

"You don't have to marry him," Chloe said. The woman knew me far too well. "But if he's offering you should at least think about having some fun with him. You've been behaving like a nun for years."

"You can talk," I shot back at her and then wished I'd kept my mouth shut as I watched a flicker of hurt cross Chloe's face.

"I'm sorry," I said, "I'm not thinking straight." It was the truth. I reached out to touch her on the arm, hopefully in some kind of reassuring way.

Chloe shrugged and clasped her hand over mine. "It's okay. It's not your fault that no-one can live up to Sam in my head. Then there's looking after Jassie and I worry about introducing her to any man. What it will do to her if he leaves." Chloe shrugged, "So many issues."

"You know that the right person will come along," I couldn't be sure how many nights I'd sat with Chloe trying to reassure her that it wasn't just going to be her and Jasmine for the rest of their lives. Besides, turning the conversation back on Chloe also meant that I didn't have to think about my increasing attraction to Harry.

I needed to stay focussed on my goal of getting overseas. The terror of being trapped in New Zealand for the rest of my life hung over me like some strange, black cloud.

"Anyway," Chloe said, "let's not talk about men. We're going out to have a great girlie night on the town. We don't need them anyway," she said a look of smug satisfaction on her face.

"I agree, they're completely overrated." I listened to the words coming out of my mouth and hoped that I sounded more convincing than I felt.

An evil grin crept across Chloe's face. "I dare you to tell Harry Pearson tomorrow night that you think he's overrated."

It's a good job we weren't sitting in a bar drinking when she said that—otherwise I'd have spat the contents of my mouth across the table.

"The Pearson family employ us both," I said, "you haven't forgotten that tiny little fact, right?"

"Of course not," I was fairly sure that Chloe's eyes twinkled with glee, or perhaps it was just the fading light and the reflection of the city's lights as we approached the downtown ferry terminal.

"Come on," she said picking up her bag and making her way towards the exit where the ferry staff would soon attach the gang plank so we could disembark. The scream of the ferry's engines turned the surrounding sea into a swirling, frothing mass as the captain threw the engines into reverse.

I couldn't imagine how many times a day he steered the massive catamaran into the wharf, but a tiny bump confirmed that he'd done it plenty of times as the boat began to settle against the hard surface. A sea of business commuters were waiting to board the ferry to take the return trip to the Island. Many did the daily commute from the Island to the city to work.

"Come on," Chloe said as she linked her arm in mine and almost pulled me towards the disembarking area. "We've got four hours before we need to be back here again. There's a noodle bar down the road with our names on a table. Let's go have some fun."

As we walked past the line of daily commuters waiting to go home, my mind turned to what Harry had said earlier in the afternoon. If he had his way, the man would be building a small city on the Island and for some reason that strategy continued to not sit well with me.

I may have been planning to escape the country to see the rest of the world, but I knew that when I came back to New Zealand, I'd still have our little home on the beachfront.

It had always been a sanctuary of sorts.

The question begged for an answer. How much of a sanctuary would it remain if Harry Pearson had his way with his plans for expansion?

"So tell me," I said to Chloe over what was left of the spicy noodles and oriental salad that remained on the table in front of us, "what goes on at a Harvest Festival?"

Chloe let out a huge burp, followed by a wide grin as she reached for the bottle of wine in the middle of the table.

"Nice not to have to drink a Pearson vintage for a change don't you think?" she asked as she topped up her glass and then tried to top up mine.

I put my hand over the top of the glass. "I need a clear head tomorrow night," I cautioned her. My stomach may well be replete from spicy noodles and a half a glass of the opposition's wine, but I wasn't about to let Chloe encourage me to drink myself into a state.

"Really?" Chloe's eyes danced with what I knew to be the anticipation of grilling me about my thoughts about the evening to come. "Tell me more about Harry Pearson. From your perspective," she added as an afterthought.

"Nothing much to tell. He's a hard worker and he's ambitious for the vineyard." I poured some iced water into the tumbler that sat beside my wine glass. As reasonable as the costs were for the dinner that we'd enjoyed, I could see why this noodle bar was doing so well. It hummed with early evening diners, many of whom would have come from the inner city apartments that now lined the backstreets of the downtown area.

From comfortable armchair-type seating, to large benches and tables for groups, the owners seemed to have struck the right chord with the locals. Good quality, reasonably priced food went a long way with people who lived in the inner city.

I thought about the plans I'd looked at on Harry's desk this afternoon and wondered whether this was the kind of atmosphere he wanted to create over on the Island. The idea continued to appall me.

"You haven't answered my question about what I can expect tomorrow night," I reminded Chloe.

"I don't see a lot from the bowels of the kitchen," she grinned at me, "as you'd recall from your lowly waitressing days."

"I've always been grateful for you getting me that job." Although I began to wonder if I should be so grateful given that I now found myself hanging around with Harry every day pretending to be some kind of personal assistant.

"And don't you forget who your friends are," Chloe said, "when you're out there tomorrow night hobnobbing it with the elite of Auckland.

I nearly spat out my water all over what was left of the food.

"Say that again."

"You heard me," she said. "The Harvest Festival is ostensibly a celebration of the end of the harvest and a chance for the Pearson's to raise some money for local charities—but really it's a PR spectacle and a chance for them to wine and dine the business people and glitterati from the Auckland social pages."

My stomach turned over.

"Maybe I will have that drink." I pushed my wine glass toward Chloe.

What the hell had I gotten myself into?

The thought never left my mind for the balance of the evening. Chloe and I caught the 10pm ferry home and I couldn't have been more pleased to see the familiar ferry waiting for us at the downtown wharf.

We'd travelled pretty much in silence. Both contemplating, no doubt, the evening ahead of us tomorrow.

There was always something comforting about getting that last ferry home, knowing that the Island was now cut off from the madness of the mainland.

I'd walked Chloe back to her house and hugged her goodbye.

"Come in for coffee?" she'd asked.

I shook my head. "No. I'll see you tomorrow."

Chloe laughed and the sound drifted down the valley. "I doubt it. You'll be too busy with the glitterati to worry about the behind-the-scenes staff."

I'd walked home pondering that thought.

At this time of the evening, after the last ferry had gone for the night back to the mainland, it struck home how quiet life on the Island really was.

It suited me, the quiet of the Island. Some people couldn't stand it. The idea that they couldn't get somewhere quickly— or that they were cut off from most of the usual services drove many of them back to the mainland.

The four and a half months that I'd been living here full time meant I was finely attuned now to the rhythm of life here.

Busy mornings.

Busy afternoons.

And these long spells of peacefulness.

How much would I miss these when I was overseas in the mayhem of the world? Even the speed that people walked on the mainland tired me out.

Maybe I wasn't as cut out for life in the city as I thought I might be?

Pondering these thoughts, I sat on the deck, a cup of comforting tea in my hand and listened to the soft swish of the waves as they washed up onto the sand.

The red or green of the odd navigational light could be seen in the distance as one or two of the weekend boaties made a decision as to whether or not they would spend the night in the Bay. Most usually decided to spend the night in the cove just north of the beach, the enclave giving them more protection from the prevailing sea breeze.

I wanted to go and lie in my familiar bed—but I knew that sleep would evade me until the early hours of the morning. Whether it was the spicy noodles, the wine or the over-stimulation of a night out with Chloe, I couldn't be sure but I was more wound up than I needed to be.

Best sit out here. It's what I'd done for years.

Who was I kidding?

Sitting out here on my own only made me think of Harry. He was the sort of man who would prefer me to be locked behind some elaborate set of electronic gates no doubt—much like the apartment blocks with their security fences and roped off area of the beach that had been built down the road.

No.

I preferred there to be nothing but a few rolling sand hills and regenerating tussock grass between me and the beach. That's the way it had been for years and that's the way that it should stay.

But Harry Pearson was the real reason that I couldn't close my eyes and go to sleep tonight.

Not for the first time, I wondered why I'd agreed to go with him to the Harvest Festival tomorrow night.

CHAPTER 9

*H*arry
I could easily have required Grace to arrive at the restaurant in time for the harvest festival, but something about her simply arriving as if she were turning up for a day at work didn't sit well with me.

For years I'd watched my father treat a plethora of various women badly. He used them and they allowed themselves to be used. The only woman I ever saw stand up to him was my own mother. Ultimately, he treated my own mother with a degree of disdain and a total lack of respect. It wasn't something that I ever aspired to do myself. In fact, I swore that I'd never turn out to be like my father—and yet there had been a string of women through my life—that needed to change.

I'd endeavoured in all of my dealings with women to treat them with the utmost respect. This was why I found myself sitting in the driveway in front of Grace Richards' home. Forefront in my mind also was the undeniable truth that I'd bribed Grace to attend the function with me.

Re-examining my motives, this single fact could easily

have been the reason for my discomfort. So, I'd decided to do the right thing and collect Grace from her home.

My logical mind assured me that by treating Grace like any other paying guest—I would be off-setting my manipulative behaviour in getting her to the event as my partner in the first place.

Logic be damned.

I had an epiphany on the short drive over to Grace's home in Spindle Bay. I wanted to see her in her own surroundings.

The little head-to-head discussion we'd had yesterday afternoon had stayed with me for over twenty-four hours now. Maybe if I spent a little time with Grace in her own home, it might give me more of an insight into what drove this intriguing woman.

Surely, something other than the offer of extra cash had encouraged her to attend tonight's annual celebration. Maybe she was community minded, I thought. Our annual celebration also acted as a local fundraiser. The profits from this year's event would be going towards fitting out the local Sea Scouts hall with much needed safety equipment and towards the purchase of two quick response quad bikes for the local ambulance service.

Driving down to Grace's home, it had not missed my attention that if the locals would quit hanging onto their old ideas and let the council widen and seal some more of the Island's roads, then we wouldn't need quad bikes for quick response situations.

As my family now owned more than a quarter of the entire land mass on Hauraki Island, we paid ridiculous sums in general rates to the council. But, despite our wealth and land ownership, we were still unable to sway the local boards to our way of thinking. Support for the members of Fish & Bird meant that progress around the Island seemed terminally slow. Many counsellors and local body politicians would be at our annual fundraiser tonight and I remained determined to sway them to my way of thinking, even if I had to persuade the vociferous and vocal opposition one-on-one.

In the meantime that did not discourage me from moving forward with my building programme plans. One way or another I would drag Hauraki Island into the new millennium. I knew I had my work cut out for me. Fish & Bird had established themselves as knights for the environment and had a huge groundswell of supporters who were determined that the Island should remain somewhere in the 1970's.

As I pulled the handbrake on outside a perfect example of early Island architecture, I could see why Fish & Bird had such a hold. As charming as the Richards' family bach had been back in its day, it was clear from the overgrown gardens and the peeling paint on the unkempt picket fence that the property had seen better times. Why the family hadn't simply accepted our offers over the years and allowed us to redevelop this prime piece of waterfront land, I couldn't fathom.

Having parked my Audi convertible on the gravel driveway, I made my way down the winding path, through garden overgrowth toward the open front door.

I knocked and waited.

Grace appeared at the front door, her hands to one ear as she finished putting the clasp on the back of a single pearl drop earring.

She wore a dark blue halter-neck dress that was pulled in at her waist and then fell to the floor. The deep colour accentuated her eyes and hugged her curves in all the right places.

A string of pearls sat at the base of her throat and she'd pulled her hair up into a tight ponytail and allowed the balance of it to fall from the top of her head to the base of her skull. With the low light from the nearly setting sun coming from behind her, she looked like an angel.

"You're early," she said, as she stood to one side and ushered me inside her home.

"Not by much," I replied as I struggled to tear my eyes away from the stunning beauty who stood in front of me.

"Twenty minutes at least," Grace said, taking on an air of authority with me that I hadn't noticed before. I could only think it came with her being in her own environment. "Come on in. There's a wine in the fridge and you can wait for me on the deck while I finish getting ready."

Having firmly been put in my place, I watched as Grace's shapely behind sashayed its way back down the hallway towards what I had to assume was her bedroom.

A part of me wanted desperately to follow her—but in view of the way I'd been greeted and then summarily dismissed—I decided that I'd best take up the offer to wait for her on the deck.

I thought about having a glass of wine, but then thought better of it. In any event, I found myself checking the fridge. I didn't want to admit it, but I was pleasantly surprised and maybe relieved to find that it was a Pearson wine that sat chilling in amongst the vegetables, assorted bottles of yoghurt and a few half eaten jars of jam.

Two comfortable looking chairs, both sporting bright green and red cushions greeted me out on the deck.

A valuable camera sat on the table. I sat down and found myself gazing out across the beach to the familiar curve of the headland at the end of Spindle Bay. It grated a little that this home sat on such a prime spot. To the left I could see right down the coast of Hauraki Island and to the right, the curve of the Bay and the tall, clay cliffs that were part of the northern headland of the island. Above those yellow cliffs and out of sight from here, hidden by the graceful trunks of the beachfront pohutukawa trees lay our northern most vineyards and my ancestral family home.

My father hadn't been the only drunken womaniser in the family. Most of Spindle Bay had at one time been owned by my ancestors, but as family history would have it, my great-great-grandfather had lost this Bay on the toss of a coin—it was something that the family never talked about. Another reason that I'd wanted to set history to rights and complete the redevelopment of the entire Bay.

I still couldn't work out why Grace's parents wouldn't accept my offer. It didn't take a genius to work out that the property was in severe need of maintenance.

Winter was coming and with it storms that would lash the front of this property with plenty of water from the ocean.

I could see where the rust marks were coming through the paint on the side of the house that bore the brunt of the salt-laden winds. Come June and July, when another winter battering hit, the stains would run further down the wood.

There were places on the deck where it looked as if the wood may well be rotted through. One step in the wrong place and someone could go right through one of the boards. Granted, we were less than three feet off the ground and hence there was no handrail blocking the view towards the sea—but still—someone could injure themselves if they fell through one of the rotten slats.

"You didn't want a wine then?" Grace appeared at my side, still a vision in the colour blue.

"No, I thought I'd wait until we got back to the vineyard. Do you always leave your valuables out here where anyone could get hold of them?" I tipped my head toward the camera sat on the table.

Grace waved her hand in a dismissive fashion. "No-one comes up here from the beach."

I couldn't be so sure. There seemed to be a complete lack of any kind of security around the bach. If it were my daughter living here alone, I'd be concerned for her safety.

Grace sat herself down next to me on the other chair. She'd come outside in bare feet.

"You are wearing shoes?"

She threw me a look that said what? I couldn't be sure.

"Of course, I'm wearing shoes. The heels are thin and I don't want to end up going through the gaps in the deck."

I pointed at the rotten looking boards. "You should be more concerned about going through the deck itself. You need to get someone here to replace those boards, or you'll have a nasty fall."

"They've been like that for years," Grace said apparently unfazed by the decrepit nature of the home she was residing in. "Shall we go?" Grace took great pains to pick up the camera from the table and then laid it on an overstuffed armchair beside the window.

"You don't subscribe to the idea of keeping valuables out of view of the window then?"

She ignored my comment. Being ignored wasn't something that I was used to.

Feeling less than in control of the situation, I followed Grace inside the main living area of the house. It disturbed me no end that this property could be so much more. Couldn't she see the potential here?

Grace pushed the bolts up into the worn wooden surrounds. She may as well simply have left the doors open, for the good those bolts were. The idea of a woman staying here on her own, with the entire front of the house open to the beach and the only thing standing between her and any kind of intruder being those inadequate bolts. Well. I didn't like it one bit.

Feeling strangely unsure of myself for the first time in my

life, I stood and watched Grace strap black and gold shoes to her feet.

For some reason, it looked as if she would have preferred to remain without shoes for the evening and I couldn't help but feel that she was making some kind of unusual concession for me.

Perhaps I wasn't alone in the disturbed nature of my thoughts and feelings tonight.

"I could send one of our locksmiths down to put some decent bolts and locks on this place," I said as Grace attended to the supposed locking of the front door.

"It's not necessary," she smiled at me. "Nothing here worth stealing."

"I'm not worried about thieves," I said as I headed back up the winding and overgrown path to my Audi convertible.

"What are you worried about then?"

"Your safety of course." I tried to keep the exasperation out of my voice. "For an intelligent woman you can be a little slow sometimes."

I pressed the lock on my keyring and the doors of the convertible clicked. I opened the passenger door for Grace.

"Thank you," she said as she slipped into the leather seat. By the time I was seated in the driver's side and I'd put on my seatbelt, Grace was staring at me with something akin to amusement on her face.

"What?" I turned the key and the Audi purred into life.

Grace nestled a black and gold evening bag in her lap. Like the bach it too looked as if it had seen better days.

"I've been coming here with my family ever since I can remember. It's perfectly safe," she said.

"It might have been ten years ago," I reminded her, "but maybe not so much now. You've seen how many people come up and down this road travelling to and from the ferry?"

"Of course." Grace snorted. "And you wonder why the community is so opposed to the kind of development that you want around here."

"I guess I left myself wide open for that one." I glanced across at the smug look painted on Grace's face.

As we made our way up the hill toward the vineyard, I began to think that I may well have met my match in a woman.

The prospect alternately excited and terrified me.

CHAPTER 10

*G*race

As the familiar circular driveway of the vineyard restaurant came into view, a sudden knot of tension gripped my stomach. I really didn't know why I'd agreed to accompany Harry to this event. From what I'd learned last night from Chloe anyone who wanted to be seen in Auckland would be here.

The last thing I wanted was to be seen by anyone in Auckland.

Keeping my head down had become an art-form for me and now I had to wonder why I'd stupidly agreed to this at all.

I couldn't help sneaking a look at Harry as we drove up to the vineyard.

The second he'd appeared at my front door I'd struggled to keep myself under control.

He wore an impeccably cut dark grey suit, over a white shirt. Before he sat himself down in the driver's seat of the convertible, he'd taken off the jacket and thrown it idly across the tiny back seat. The flawless white shirt hugged his body in all the right places.

A dark blue tie was held in place with a thick, gold tiepin that bore the crest of the Pearson vineyard.

Harry had been nothing less than perfectly turned out each day during working hours, but this took his attraction level from boiling to scalding.

My body had begun to tremble the closer we got to the vineyard. It had nothing to do with the way Harry threw the Audi around the tight bends in the road and everything to do with the smouldering heat of the sexual attraction I could feel suspended between the two of us.

I'd done some silly things in my life, but agreeing to come to this dinner with Harry may well have topped every other disastrous decision I'd made.

Harry drove right past the front door of the restaurant where I caught a glimpse of the milling crowd.

"Isn't the function in the restaurant?" I asked as we continued on down the vineyard driveway and past the sign marked, "Private Property" to where I knew the main residence was located.

"It is," Harry said as he flicked a quick glance in my direction. He'd slowed the Audi as we drove through the tall Puriri trees that lined the entranceway all the way to the house beyond. "But I never like to get to one of these events too early, so I thought we might have a drink at the house beforehand. Get to know each other a little better."

Was I hearing him right?

The idea of being alone with Harry Pearson in his home set my heart beating at a rapid rate.

"Unless of course," he said eyeing me with an evil grin as he brought the car to a stop at the top of the driveway, "you'd rather be circulating with the politicians and businessmen who've come to sample our hospitality for the evening?"

"No," I stammered. Now I could see why he'd stopped at

the top of the driveway. He wanted me to be able to take in the view of the house below.

Well, if you could call it a house.

Rumours about the grandeur of the Pearson estate abounded around the Island. Like British royalty, anyone who worked inside the house or in any domestic capacity with the family were bound by a gag-clause in their employment contract.

Over the years, the odd photograph of the exterior had found its way into the press, or onto the internet, but to see the property now. In its entirety. From the top of the hill.

I didn't know what to say.

It wasn't only being in the presence of Harry Pearson that could take my breath away.

"Welcome to Ridgedale," Harry said as he put the Audi into gear and prepared to begin the descent to the front of the impressive building.

The imposing white stone of the front of the family home came into view. Behind it, from what I'd heard or read about on the internet, I knew stood long wings of the home where multiple generations of the family had resided.

I thought of the old car packing cases that lined the walls of my family bach. We had our own family history here, but it didn't run as far back as the Pearson family history.

Generations of the same family had lived inside the wings of this impressive structure. Like Harry and his brothers they left the Island, but then they returned to take their rightful place inside this very building.

Beyond the white bleached stone of the facade, the familiar lines of the vines ran toward the private beach and the Hauraki Gulf beyond.

To be here. To actually be allowed to see the property that had housed generations of the Pearson family.

My mouth went dry.

Harry wanted to take me inside.

I hadn't signed any kind of gag order. The only document that I'd ever signed had been an employment agreement.

It ran through my mind whether or not there was anything inside that contract that would prevent me from talking about what I saw here now.

As difficult as it was to drag my eyes from the manicured lawns and the edges of the perfectly clipped box hedges that circled the fountain in the middle of the driveway, I cast a glance at Harry.

He had stopped the car and was watching my reaction.

A small curve at the corner of his mouth, the only indication that he was enjoying what must have been a maelstrom of emotion crossing my face.

"It's just a house," he said as he let the brake go on the Audi and we cruised effortlessly around the circular driveway.

"Not like any kind of house I've ever seen," I said and then added, "and one that you're at pains to keep out of the news. Are you going to make me sign a gag order before I leave?"

Harry laughed.

The warmth of the sound eased the tension that I hadn't even realised I'd been carrying in my body.

Harry turned the Audi to the left and took us around the back of the building, we left the fountain and the front entrance of the building behind us. Then Harry said his tone full of warmth, "I trust you, Grace. It's been my experience that, except for the mistake she made with my father, my mother is a great judge of character."

I didn't know how to respond.

It was the first time that Harry had mentioned his father. He must have known it was common knowledge the way his father had behaved and his ancestors before him.

Hell.

His younger brother was never out of the news.

A sudden thought hit me.

What made Harry Pearson so different from the generations of Pearson men who had come before him?

I pulled my pashmina a little closer around me, the soft wool caressing my skin and giving me some comfort. I needed to keep my head with this man.

"So you bring all of your personal assistants back here?"

"No," Harry replied as he pulled the Audi to a stop in front of one of four long wings of the house that extended out from the rear of the building. He turned to face me, the piercing aqua blue of his eyes drilling into me. "We can go back up to the vineyard if you'd rather not come here for a drink with me."

A sudden rush of heat through my body had me rethinking my decision to cloak myself in the fine wool.

He was giving me an out.

Forcing me to make the decision as to whether or not we went inside for a drink. I could stop this right now. Whatever *this* was becoming. I could spend the evening by Harry Pearson's side. Be introduced as his PA and then come back to work on Monday morning and nothing would have changed.

I could feel the beat of my heart pulsing at the base of my neck.

The air stilled and a heavy silence hung between us as Harry waited for me to make my decision. I could hear the distant sound of the waves as they crashed on the shore at the beach below. The familiar sound of the gulls calling each other to their evening roost.

Harry didn't blink.

Didn't say a word.

The scent of him washed around me.

Musk and sandalwood with the promise of hot sex.

Still, he said nothing. Simply waited for me to make my decision.

Harry Pearson terrified me.

My heart beat faster. The rational side of my brain fought to make itself heard above the screeching call of my libido.

I should have taken him up on his offer to drive us back to the vineyard restaurant. Instead I heard me say, "A drink would be nice, thank you."

Harry

I couldn't be sure what had come over me.

Inviting Grace back up to my apartment wasn't part of my plan for the evening and it would certainly piss my mother off us arriving late.

For some reason, I didn't care. It seemed right to bring her here to my sanctuary.

Maybe I'd invited her in because she'd seemed so comfortable having me at her home?

That didn't make sense.

Nothing about Grace made sense.

I'd come back to Hauraki Island six months ago with a deep distrust of women and I'd made a decision that I wouldn't allow myself to get close to anyone and yet, here I found myself, inextricably attracted to a woman who had lived on this Island for nearly as long as me.

How had I never seen her before?

Had I too been guilty of casting my eyes out to the world stage and overlooking the wonder that lay here right on my doorstep?

As I punched the code into the lock on the door of my suite, I could feel Grace's eyes on me.

For some strange reason, I'd taken extra care when I

dressed tonight. For the first time in an age, it wasn't simply my mother that I wanted to please.

I hadn't missed the sly glances that Grace had been giving me on the drive to the vineyard. It was the reason that I'd eventually decided to take a detour to the house.

Mother wouldn't be happy—but for some reason that didn't bother me tonight.

All I wanted to do was get Grace alone, in my own environment.

I knew there was no chance we'd be disturbed.

All the staff were at the event.

My two twin brothers were overseas and Seb had already escorted Mother to the vineyard.

At best, we had an hour.

An hour alone with Grace.

My body fairly vibrated in her presence.

I pushed the heavy kauri door open and ushered Grace into the sanctuary which was my ancestral home.

"Upstairs," I said, gesturing with my hand toward the rimu staircase that led to the living quarters on the first floor.

Grace started up the stairs, the clip of her heels on the wooden boards the only sound that filled the space.

"I didn't expect it to be so modern," Grace said as she reached the loft-like living space at the top of the stairs.

"Each of these wings were built to accommodate various families over the generations," I explained as I found a couple of glasses. "Red or white?"

"Whatever you want," Grace replied as she surveyed the view from the large open window that faced out to the gulf. "You get amazing views from up here."

I pulled a cold half bottle of champagne out of the fridge and popped the cork. The sound made Grace jump and she pulled her white shawl tighter around her shoulders.

"Are you cold?" I kept the apartment at a comfortable level, but I could always turn the heat up—one way or another—if Grace was cold.

She turned to face me and let the fine woollen shawl fall from the bend of her arms. "No. A little nervous, perhaps."

The admission shook me and I hesitated for a moment pouring the wine.

"Nervous?" I handed Grace a champagne flute and we touched the tips of the flutes together. Our eyes never left each other as we took a sip of the tangy liquid.

"Chloe tells me that there will be a lot of important people at dinner tonight?"

"Chloe?"

"She's one of your kitchen hands. We pretty much grew up here together."

"How did I miss you for all these years?" I gestured for Grace to take a seat on one of the Starck couches that sat opposite each other in front of the large windows.

"I guess I was only here for the holidays. I was schooled out west where mum and dad live and then I went on to university."

"That makes sense." What didn't make sense was why I had Grace here at all. What was it about this intriguing creature that stirred so many deep emotions in me and so quickly?

Mother had been trying to match-make with me for years —maybe if I'd taken some notice, I wouldn't have had such an unfortunate experience in Italy.

"You have no reason to be nervous, Grace," I said. I liked the sound of her name. The way it rolled of my tongue. "I'll look after you. If you have any trouble with anyone tonight, or any time at all, you can call on me."

I watched in fascination as the colour began to creep up Grace's face.

I knew she felt the crackling attraction between us.

"Shouldn't we be getting on?" Grace asked as she looked past me to the clock that I knew sat on the wall behind me.

"There's plenty of time," I lied.

It wasn't that I didn't want to go to the function, more that I wanted to spend more time than we had here, alone, getting to know Grace.

I'd finished my glass of champagne. I didn't drink this fast. I had to pace myself. I had to do something. Just sitting here beside Grace was driving me crazy.

All I wanted to do was slip the thin strap of her dress from her shoulder. Explore the soft, milky white flesh that led to the curve of her breast.

Drinking any more champagne wouldn't keep my head straight.

In fact, having a glass had probably set my mind on this tangent.

Who was I kidding?

I'd been set on this tangent from the first moment I'd set eyes on Grace.

She was in trouble.

And I was digging myself in deeper and deeper with every passing moment.

CHAPTER 11

*G*race
Harry had finished his glass of champagne.

I'd barely touched mine.

My head swam simply being alone in the same room with him.

The distraction of work had been fine.

But now.

This.

Here in his apartment.

Alone.

I couldn't keep my eyes from his body.

The cut of his shirt.

The slant of his jaw.

The way that he moved with such assurance and confidence.

How had I allowed myself to be brought back here? To be alone with him?

The man was dangerous.

Dangerous in the most attractive way. The small, feisty voice in my brain whispered.

I could feel the heat and tension in my body as it increased with each moment that passed.

Every time he'd put his glass to his lips and taken a sip of champagne I'd wondered what it would feel like to kiss those full lips.

I'd watched his hands circle the wine bottle, his strong fingers hold the delicate wine glass.

I wanted those hands on my body.

I ached to be caressed by this strong and virile man.

Nothing had prepared me for the way I'd feel tonight.

Here with him.

I'd stupidly thought that I could keep him at a distance. That the relationship we had at work would somehow protect me from the call of his masculine grace.

Now was the time to admit that I had been wrong.

I stood up.

I needed to put some space between us.

Another roll of plans sat sprawled across the dining table not more than five feet from where we'd sat on the couch.

I walked over.

Started to look at the plans.

Maybe if I turned my mind to the work that we were doing together, then I could ignore the increasing tension growing in my body.

I thumbed through the plans. "Are these the same set we have in the office?" I asked, casually trying to bring my mind back to work and away from the heat of the body that had sat beside me on the couch.

Maybe I should have kept the question to myself.

"No," Harry said leaning in and looking over my shoulder at the plans spread across the smoked glass of the table.

"This is a plan of the replica Italian castle that I plan to build on the furthest northern site," he said as he pointed to the sketch drawing on the table, effectively encasing me in the alcove of his hard body. As he spoke the words, I could feel the heat of his breath on the back of my neck. My nipples turned to tight little nubs under my dress and my body began to tremble.

"You are cold," Harry murmured as he took my glass and put it down on the table.

"No. Like I said before. I'm fine," I tried to assure him. To my horror and delight, I felt his arms slip around my body.

I sucked in a breath.

"I could warm you up," he growled in my ear.

As his lips touched the side of my neck, half of me wanted to panic and the other half screamed for more.

By this point I may as well have been having and out-of-body experience. I heard someone moan and then realised it was me.

My body went onto auto-pilot.

Some kind of carnal monster that had been residing deep inside of me heaved a breath of life and unleashed herself.

Whether it was the wine. Harry, or where I stood, I couldn't be sure, but I abandoned all pretence of caution and threw my head back against Harry's chest allowing him access to the full length of my neck.

Harry didn't need a written invitation. His hands began to explore and my body quivered in response to his touch.

Tiny butterfly kisses tickled their way up and down the side of my neck.

Strong hands found their way from my waist to my ample breasts.

As Harry palmed each breast in turn, a flood of heat ran through me.

I swallowed my mouth dry and my lips eager for the taste of his.

Harry turned me around and raked his eyes across me.

Desire burned in his hooded eyes.

With infinite care, he took my face in his hands, tilted it up towards his and said, "I've wanted to do this from the moment I helped you up off the floor."

His lips were on mine.

An overwhelming sense of coming home swept through me.

I opened my mouth and allowed his insistent tongue access.

Harry's hand found its way under my dress and my skin burned at his touch. He crushed me to him in another smothering kiss and I thought that my legs would collapse from under me.

"Do you want me?" The question came in a rush of passion.

"Yes," I gasped.

Harry lifted me up on the large table and I sucked in a breath as the cool glass bit at my skin. He pushed me back down on top of the plans, all thought of an Italian castle lost in the sea of growing heat that rose between us.

"You're sure?" Harry asked, his voice thick with desire.

"Yes," I heard myself say. I'd never wanted anyone the way I wanted Harry Pearson in that moment.

He pulled my dress aside and pulled the thin scrap of cotton that were my panties down to my ankles. He stopped at my feet and with great care unbuckled my sandals and removed them before slipping the cotton from my legs.

Sitting up on the table, half undressed, my legs spread wide for Harry I felt alternatively vulnerable and alive.

Harry murmured his approval as I felt the gentle scraping of his tightly trimmed beard against my inner thighs.

I should have gotten up off that table, but I wanted his mouth on me. I wanted his tongue inside of me the way it had been inside my mouth. As he licked his way up my inner thighs, my body began to quiver in anticipation of his touch.

He slipped a finger inside of me. I moaned and arched up off the table.

"So very wet for me," Harry said as his tongue slid across my clit.

I began to pant.

He continued to finger me and to lick me until I didn't think I could stand it any longer.

A raging heat began to beat from my body. I could feel myself climbing higher and higher. Pleasure coursed through me and I had an uncontrollable feeling of speeding somewhere and being unable to stop.

I could feel my muscles pulsing around Harry's thick fingers as his lips and tongue continued their dance against my sensitive flesh.

"That's right," he said, "I want you to come big for me."

My breath came in short, harsh pants and my entire body felt as if it were about to explode.

"Come on," Harry coaxed, "come for me baby."

At the sound of his words, I could stand it no longer. Something inside of me snapped and my entire body was taken by a wave of pleasure that I'd never experienced in the presence of a man before.

"Good girl," he cooed, as he slid his hips between my legs and leaned in to kiss me.

A flush of heat raced across my chest as Harry's mouth, sweet with my juices, came down again on mine. I kissed him hungrily, acknowledging the heat of his own desire as he continued to caress my soaked pussy.

"I can't wait to fuck you good and proper," he growled.

I wanted him to fuck me now.

As if answering my thoughts, he said, "Later, babe. We have to be somewhere. But I promise you this," he said as he kissed me gently again, "the next time you come you're going to be calling my name."

Another shiver ran through my body.

Somewhere in the fog of my mind I heard a cellphone ring.

"Shit, it's Kathryn," Harry said. "I'm sorry I have to take this." He began to walk away and then stopped and turned around. "I approve of the view. Any chance you can be waiting for me like that on my desk on Monday?"

I realised I was still laying splayed out on his dining table my legs apart. I hurriedly sat up and pulled my dress around me. I scanned the floor and located my shoes, but my panties seemed to have vanished.

"Mother," Harry said into his phone. Then I watched in horror as he wiped his face with my panties, held them to his nose and then put them in his suit pocket.

He spoke at length with his mother on the phone. I scarcely heard a word. All I could think was that I stood there soaked in my own juices and now I had to go and face his family.

I put my sandals back on, all the while wondering what the hell I'd gotten myself into.

One week ago I thought I had a clear path set for my life. Then Harry Pearson had stepped in, knocked me to the floor and it seemed my head hadn't stopped spinning since.

*H*arry

I wasn't in the habit of stealing panties from young women, but there was something about Grace that intrigued me in a way that I'd never been intrigued by a woman before.

I simply couldn't get enough of her.

The scent of Grace's arousal lingered on the panties that I'd brazenly stolen. The look on her face as I'd walked away with them in my hand had been worth it.

The telephone discussion with Kathryn had left me with the worst case of lover's balls.

"Mother is waiting for us," I said to Grace as she stood looking sheepish on the other side of the room. "The bathroom is through the hallway and to the left, if you'd like to freshen up."

"I would, thank you," she replied. I picked up her evening bag and handed it to her. Grace took it from me and hesitated for a moment. She had a post-orgasmic glow.

Her lips were full.

Her hair, while not completely disheveled had a just-ravaged look about it that I liked.

I wondered what she would look like waking up next to me.

"Is there anything else?" I asked.

"M-my panties…"

I couldn't keep the broad grin from my face. "They're mine now. I'm afraid I won't be giving them back."

A fresh flush of colour rose up Grace's face.

"But, I can't go out like this."

"Oh, but you can," I said as I cradled Grace's chin in my hand before I laid a soft kiss on her lips. Then I whispered, "If I can go out with the scent of you across my face, then you can go out without your underwear."

She turned and headed for the bathroom and I swatted her backside with my hand to send her on her way.

I may have been mistaken, but I thought I heard a small groan of pleasure come from Grace as she walked toward the bathroom.

While she was gone fixing herself up, I tidied away the champagne flutes and made sure that the apartment was in order. All the while trying to work out how fast we could make our exit from the festival and be back here.

My balls ached.

They were going to ache all night until I could get my cock inside of Grace.

I hadn't planned on feeling this way about a woman. Everything about Grace had taken me by surprise.

The way she stood up to me.

The beautiful curve of her body.

The scent of her.

The way she trembled at my touch.

Like a fine wine, a taste of her had made me crave more.

I knew that I wouldn't be happy until I had that woman in my bed screaming my name while she came.

race
I leaned against the marble vanity top in the sumptuously appointed bathroom. Out of sight of Harry for the first time this evening, it came home to me exactly what I'd gotten myself into.

My backside still smarted where he'd tapped me on my way.

A promise of things to come?

Harry Pearson liked to be in control.

That much was obvious from the way he'd pocketed my panties.

I knew that I could walk out of this bathroom and ask to be taken home and he would take me. He may be a man set on getting what he wanted out of life—but he made certain that I was a willing participant before satisfying my desires.

My body shivered again at the memory of his touch.

Who was I kidding?

I didn't want to go home.

I didn't exactly want to go to the harvest festival—but I

knew that once I'd attended the function with Harry, we both had it in our minds that we'd come back here.

I cleaned myself up.

Touched up my hair and make-up.

Checked myself again in the mirror.

Took a deep breath and opened the door.

Harry was leaning up against the bar in the kitchen. He looked up as he heard me enter the room. An even smile spread across his face and travelled to his eyes. Every atom in my body bloomed in response.

"You look beautiful," he purred, "I may have been remiss in telling you that earlier tonight."

I couldn't help myself. Somehow I stood a little taller under the caress of his words.

Harry offered me his arm and I slipped mine through his and allowed him to escort me down the stairs to the waiting Audi.

"My panties?" I tried again, as he prepared to close the passenger door on me.

"Like I said before, they're mine now," he replied as he shut the door and then patted his pocket.

I guess that was the end of that conversation.

If I was honest, the idea of going out with my underwear in Harry's pocket—like everything about Harry—part thrilled me and part terrified me.

Harry's hand found its way to my thigh and he gave me a reassuring squeeze. "You know that I'd never force you to do anything you're not comfortable with, don't you, Grace?"

I thought it a strange question. "Of course."

"I'll push your boundaries."

"I can see that," I said as I wriggled in the car seat. I was unaccustomed to going out in public without underwear. But somehow it seemed risqué—like everything about Harry.

"But you need to tell me if I really overstep them."

I nodded.

"I mean it." He said suddenly sounding very serious.

"Don't worry," I replied. "I'll let you know when you've gone too far."

"Good," he said as he gunned the Audi into life and we headed for the vineyard restaurant and the harvest festival.

*H*ow many times had I crossed the threshold of this building? Yet, tonight I could feel the tension rising inside of me as we approached the familiar entranceway to the vineyard restaurant.

The inside of the building had been decked out to look like some kind of Greek amphitheatre.

Clearly, no expense had been spared.

The familiar arrangement of wine barrels that adorned the wall of the cave-like structure had been replaced with stone pillars. Out of naked curiosity and in as subtle a way as possible, I managed to touch one of them. From the temperature and texture of the material, it became obvious that they were some kind of hard foam that had been painted over to look like stone.

Large vans were parked out the back of the vineyard, in the adjacent parking area, emblazoned with the logo of one of the prominent event organisers in Auckland. The company had outdone themselves, turning the vineyard restaurant into the home of Greek Gods.

Large beams crossed the ceiling where the fairy-lights usually ran and across each beam layers of vines and grapes had been hung. It felt as if we were standing in amongst the acres of vines themselves.

Kathryn approached us and if she hadn't stopped to greet another guest on her way, I would barely have recognised Harry's mother. Gone were her regulation jeans and shirt, with her hair tied up in a tight bun on her head. She looked resplendent in a long black gown, with a collar of diamonds at her neck. In the centre of the sparkling stones sat the most amazing violet amethyst. Whether it was the way she was dressed, or the way her hair framed her face and softened her features, she looked all together as if a couple of decades had vanished overnight.

"Harry, darling," she said as she allowed her son to kiss her on each cheek, "and Grace, it's so good to see you." She clasped my hand like I was some kind of long, lost friend, not a waitress that she'd sent to work for her son not much more than a week ago.

"Come," she said turning her attention back to Harry, "I want you to speak with the Mayor and his deputy. I think it will be good for you to be on first name terms." She struck out ahead of us and I watched in shock as Harry fell into line and followed his mother across the room. A quick look across his shoulder and a tilt of his chin, I presumed to be an indication that I should follow.

Without any kind of hesitation, I trotted after them both, terrified to remain standing in the spot at the entranceway to the restaurant alone. Somehow I'd lost a sense of my place in this environment.

Wherever I looked, familiar faces from television and the internet smiled and nodded towards us as Kathryn parted the crowd and we slipped through the middle of the fashionably dressed men and women.

Harry appeared totally at ease with these people and shook a hand here, or greeted someone by name there. Dumbstruck, I followed in the wake of the Pearson matriarch and her eldest son.

Stephanie, a girl who I'd worked the floor with arrived at our side, a silver tray of champagne in her hand. When she offered the tray to me, the smile that had been on her face fell to a grim line.

"Hi," I said relief flooding through me at seeing someone that I knew arrive in my vicinity. We'd gotten on reasonably well when we worked the floor together.

Stephanie stared through me as if I didn't exist.

My stomach lurched.

She stood still and waited for me to take a glass—not even treating me with the respect that we'd been trained to treat all guests with at the vineyard.

My hand trembled as I took a glass of the offered champagne from the tray.

I watched with growing horror as Stephanie, once my friend and working companion, without saying a word, turned her back on me before offering her tray, complete with a smile, to the person standing to my left.

Harry to my right was deep in conversation with Kathryn and the Mayor. Introductions had been made, but somehow the Mayor and his wife were more interested in speaking to Harry and Kathryn.

Why the hell had I agreed to come at all?

After Stephanie was far enough away that she would not have been able to overhear the conversation, I heard a voice whisper in my ear, "What did you do to piss her off?"

At least someone was speaking to me. I assumed it was another one of the staff who were circulating with trays of tiny, delicious treats. The way my stomach felt at the moment, there would be little chance of me enjoying any of the expensive morsels on offer.

It took me a few moments to compose myself and turn towards the source of the question. I was shocked to discover that the voice didn't, in fact, belong to another member of the staff, but that it belonged to Sebastian Pearson.

I recognised him in an instant.

Not because I knew the man—far from it. But because of all the Pearson brothers he was the notorious one. Seb was always in the headlines for one reason or another. Not so much in the way his late father had been in the headlines— more because he was a headstrong young man who seemed determined to make some kind of name for himself.

It always appeared to me that Seb had a great need to prove that he was as good, or even better, than his three brothers.

Stood beside me, in a suit not unlike the one sported by his brother, Harry, Seb seemed at ease with everyone around him.

Why shouldn't he be at ease?

Like his three brothers, Seb had been brought up to circulate with these kinds of people. He was firmly ensconced with his tribe.

Me on the other hand.

A shudder ran over my body and, again it wasn't because I was cold.

No.

It was because I was an outsider here.

I no longer fit.

Anywhere!

I wasn't part of the glitterati and now neither, according to the cold shoulder treatment that I'd received at the hands of Stephanie, was I part of the waiting staff.

I found myself in some kind of limbo land.

"I don't think we've met," Seb said, holding out his hand to me. "I'm Sebastian Pearson, but you can call me, Seb."

I took his offered hand and tried not to look ridiculously grateful for the fact that he'd even struck up a conversation with me.

"I'm Grace Richards," I replied, trying to keep the quiver out of my voice.

"My brother's date for the evening," Seb said, never dropping eye contact, but releasing his firm grip on my hand. "I saw the two of you come in. Kathryn's my date," he peered over my shoulder, "but it looks as if we have both been abandoned in favour of trying to sway the council on my brother's Island improvements."

Seb leaned in and whispered to me in a conspiring tone, "To be honest, I hate these kinds of things, but we're all obliged to be here."

I gave him a weak smile. Should I tell him that, in fact, I wasn't actually his brother's date? That I was here as a hired hand.

"So Harry tells me that you're working for him?"

No need to worry about that then. "Yes," I nodded. "I was working here in the restaurant, but he wanted someone to help out with his projects and your mother suggested me."

"Ah," Seb lifted his chin, "Now I get it," he said with a touch of a smile. The smile and the warmth in his voice put me more at ease and I took a sip of the champagne that I'd been holding onto like a life preserver.

"Get what?"

"Mother keeps a firm reign on what goes on around here. She must have thought that you'd be a good fit for Harry."

My mind wandered to the vision of Harry kneeling between my legs not less than half an hour ago. The fact that I stood here with an ensemble of the who's who of Auckland and I wore no panties. I could feel the heat crawling up my face. I hoped that wasn't the kind of fit that Seb was talking about.

"Don't worry," Seb said, leaning in to me. "The both of them, their bark is worse than their bite."

Was he playing with me?

Maybe this all some kind of ridiculous Pearson brother joke.

I felt an arm slide around my waist. Harry appeared at my side, his touch instantly putting me at ease.

"Seb," he said acknowledging the presence of his sibling. "I trust that my youngest brother has introduced himself," Harry said tightening his grip around my waist.

"Yes," Seb replied, "we were just discussing our mutual abandonment issues, with you and mother so focussed on keeping our guests happy."

Seeing the two brothers side by side, it became apparent how physically different they were.

Harry and the twins could almost be triplets, but Seb, with his fair hair and green eyes seemed to take more after his mother than his three older brothers.

"You know what she's like," Harry said.

"Well, she was pretty down on you for taking your time to get here."

"Couldn't be helped," Harry said as he gave me a gentle squeeze.

Seb gestured towards the table at the head of the room. "It looks as if Kathryn's about ready to get this dog and pony show on the road." He took my hand and brushed my knuckles with his lips. "It was nice to meet with you, Grace. No doubt I'll be seeing more of you in the future." He bowed his head in a formal way that I'd not expected. "But if you'll excuse me. I'm here with Kathryn and now I'm needed."

I watched as Seb made his way across the room to where his mother stood behind what appeared to be a large, stone bench.

"Ladies and gentlemen," Seb said speaking into a microphone that sat atop the bench. "On behalf of Kathryn Pearson and the entire Pearson family, I'd like to welcome you to the vineyard tonight to celebrate the harvest of this year's vintage."

It seemed strange to me that Harry as the eldest son wouldn't be welcoming everyone to the function.

"If you'd like to take your allocated seats, we will be serving shortly. Then later on in the evening, my dear brother, Harry will be outlining the plans we have for the vineyard."

That answered my question.

All heads turned in our direction. I wanted to crawl under the nearest table. How did everyone know exactly where Harry stood in the room?

Seb continued, "And please don't forget the silent auction we have going in the annex. There are plenty of wonderful prizes to be bid on and all the money raised is going to great causes."

There was a resounding sound of applause around the room.

"So please, take your seats and enjoy the hospitality."

Another round of applause and I felt Harry's hand in the small of my back.

"Where are we sitting?" I asked hoping that it was away in a corner somewhere.

"On the top table," he replied.

Again, I wondered why I'd agreed to put myself through this. Stephanie wasn't the only member of staff looking through me like I didn't exist.

Or was my imagination running away with me?

CHAPTER 13

*G*race

It was a strange feeling, being waited on by the staff instead of waiting on the patrons.

In all the months that I'd been working for the Pearson family I'd never once dined in the establishment itself. If I'd eaten here, it was out in the service yard behind the kitchen, in amongst the plastic trays that foodstuffs were delivered in.

Tonight, my peers had done away with their usual jeans and were dressed in all black. I hadn't imagined the animosity pouring off my old workmates. I couldn't help but feel the scathing looks from people that I'd once worked with as they served my food.

To make matters worse, I sat at the head table with the Pearson family. For a fleeting moment I'd thought about suggesting to Harry that I hide away in a corner, but I didn't think he'd have been happy with that suggestion.

Not for the first time this evening, I wished that I'd never accepted Harry's invitation to be a part of what his brother had described as a *dog and pony show*.

But then Harry's fingers would touch my thigh, or I'd

squeeze them together and I remembered the heat of him. The way his lips and fingers played me and a rush of something pleasurable that I couldn't quite articulate would run through me.

"Are you okay?" Harry asked in a break from one of the long and involved discussions he was having with his mother.

I'd forced myself to eat, despite feeling incredibly out of my depth and my emotions running on a constant roller coaster. I continued to push a small portion of venison around my plate.

Chloe and the team had put together a stunning menu for the event. We'd already been served an aromatic seafood chowder, followed by crayfish with caviar. My appetite hadn't quite left me, but all the time that I enjoyed the food and the service I somehow felt as if I were being disloyal to the people that I'd formerly worked alongside. Sitting up here with the owners of the establishment, it was clear that I'd crossed some kind of indistinguishable line and I didn't feel good about it.

I needed to confide in someone. Harry was the only person sitting alongside me. "The waiting staff. They hate me being here," I whispered.

"Who?" He asked. The tone of his voice told me everything I needed to know.

I should have kept my mouth shut. What was I thinking? He'd have them fired.

A little voice in my head sang:

An Audi.

A glass of champagne.

One orgasm and you've forgotten everything about who you are and where you've come from.

I shook my head. "It's me, I'm overreacting."

His hand found its way to my thigh again and the tension

instantly eased from my body. I hadn't realised how uptight I had become until the angst slipped away.

Being here.

With the Pearson family.

On show.

The prospect of trying to make small talk with the dozens of heads of business who had attended the harvest festival, it had all taken its toll. That's aside from the fallout of the feelings I was dealing with from my interlude with Harry in his apartment.

When I thought about it why did I worry about what the wait staff were thinking? Especially when Harry's own mother and brother had greeted me with such warmth.

I sliced off a piece of the tender venison and savoured the sweet taste. Harry's hand sat, warm and comforting on my thigh while he continued in conversation with his mother.

What would Chloe tell me to do? I thought I knew the answer to that question, she'd tell me to get over myself and enjoy the moment. Besides, I was going away in a few weeks. Who cared what my former workmates thought? Most of them were probably jealous and would happily exchange places with me.

Stephanie arrived and filled up my water glass.

"Thank you, Steph," I said with the warmest tone of voice I could muster and I added a sweet smile.

"You're welcome," she said as she returned my smile.

I must be making progress, I thought to myself and then I caught sight of the look on Harry's face. Stephanie wasn't making any kind of exception for me—she knew Harry was watching her.

"Okay?" Harry asked, squeezing my thigh again.

"Perfect," I replied.

If I kept telling myself that then maybe things would be perfect.

*H*arry

Having Grace at my side all evening made what would usually be an unbearable function bearable.

All I had to do was reach across under the table and surreptitiously touch her thigh and a flash of memory relieved the interminable boredom of another evening spent making small talk with people I'd ordinarily rather avoid in a social setting.

The sooner we could get the balance of the evening out of the way and I could get Grace back to my apartment—where I could start where I had left off—the better as far as I was concerned.

It disturbed me the way that the wait staff had been treating Grace. She thought I hadn't noticed, but there was very little that I missed. It was a skill that I'd inherited from my mother and one that had stood me in good stead for quite some time.

Dessert had been served and eaten and the scent of freshly brewed coffee filled the room as large silver urns of the aromatic liquid were carried from table to table.

Our waitress appeared again and this time I watched with a degree of satisfaction as she treated Grace with the same hospitality that we'd come to expect our staff to treat all our guests.

I knew that I'd crossed some kind of line with Grace—but after the early part of this evening—I didn't care.

Mother appeared to be quite taken with her and that was enough for me.

Seb seemed a little too happy to keep Grace entertained while I'd circulated between courses with mother. Every time I vacated my seat, he moved into it and, whenever I looked back to catch Grace's eye, she seemed to be in deep conversation with him.

My brother may have a reputation as a playboy—but I trusted him. I also knew he was ensuring that the family hospitality was maintained by keeping my partner entertained while I dealt with other family duties.

I would have trusted any of my brothers with my life.

While father had been at the helm of the family, the four of us had stood shoulder-to-shoulder with our mother. We gave her our one hundred percent support and nothing had changed since the death of the old man.

The third time I looked back, I did manage to catch Grace's eye. Even from where I stood, I could see the flush of joy on her face as she sent a beaming grin back across the room—just for me.

If it wasn't for the fact that we had so many people attending this evening's festivities who had a vested interest in making sure that my plans for the vineyard went ahead, I might have abandoned the idea of remaining any longer. The more time I spent with Grace, the more enticing a creature she became. Her obvious joy at having spotted me from across the room made me want to escape my duties and take her back to my apartment.

In fact, I could scarcely stand to be away from her for another moment. "If you'll excuse me," I said to mother and Geoff McDonnell, the head of the city's business development team.

"Of course, Harry," mother said as she touched a hand to my arm, "You've been neglecting Grace long enough."

The woman could read my mind, I was certain.

Less than a metre away from the table, I was accosted by the Mayor.

"Harry, if I could have a moment,"

"Certainly," I hid the irritation from my voice at being stopped from reaching Grace.

"I've been thinking about your plans for putting another

wharf at Spindle Bay."

Now he did have my attention. It had been a pet project of mine for quite some time. Along with the caves and the plans for the piazza, a new wharf was integral to expansion plans.

"As we've explained," I said trying to make sure that I got my point home, "A wharf at the northern most tip of Spindle Bay would accommodate the increasing numbers we would need to accommodate in the piazza and it would segue well with the accommodation we already have built on the beach-front. Private access to this and the northern parts of the Island are one of the great selling points." I had this patter down, but it didn't hurt for the Mayor to hear it again. "We plan to deliver on this as part of our promise to bring more exclusive patrons to the Island."

The Mayor nodded, "Yes, I can see that it would be of assistance. As you know," he said moving in towards me and lowering the tone of his voice, "my term will be coming to an end in the next eighteen months. I like the look of what you're doing with the Island and my dear wife," I followed his gaze and saw the Mayoress deep in conversation with a couple of the members of the council's planning committee, "loves the conceptual drawings that have come across her desk from your architectural team."

It hadn't escaped my notice that the Mayoress had declined giving up her day job and still held some influence with the council's planning committee. She was the kind of woman I admired—much like my mother—she'd worked hard, beginning as a draughts woman in a city architectural firm and then working her way to a degree and head of a prestigious architectural firm.

Her influence could be seen in many of the large, corporate towers that now dominated the city's skyline.

"You mean your lovely wife would be prepared to give up all the glamour of city life and come and live here?" These were the kind of endorsements that I knew would eventually skyrocket the project and have people flocking to live here.

He nodded. "Jocelyn's extremely impressed with the light and space that she sees in the concept drawings. In fact, she'd be more than willing to lend a hand if needed."

"I'll keep that in mind," I said, "but the wharf?" Now I knew what the quid pro quo involved, it was time to bring the Mayor back to the tricky question of consent and approval for a new wharf at the northern tip of Spindle Bay.

He leaned back from me and raised his tone. "I think the new wharf would be a great addition to the Island and I'll be advising Council of my thoughts on the matter at our next meeting."

"Excellent," that was what I wanted to hear. "Tell Jocelyn that I'll set up a meeting with her next week to discuss her thoughts on the piazza."

We shook hands. The deal done.

"She'll be thrilled to hear that you'd like her to take a look," the Mayor said.

I'm sure she will. I thought as I made my way back to Grace.

The warm smile that had drawn me here from the other side of the room was gone. In its place a grim line and tight lips.

"You're planning to put another wharf at Spindle Bay?" Grace's tone told me that this was not news well received.

"At the headland. It won't affect the beach where your property sits."

"The hell it won't," Grace replied her voice rising with each word. "Were you planning to let the locals know about this?"

"Keep your voice down." There was a comfortable buzz in the room, but I didn't need or want Grace making a scene.

"I will not be silenced."

I took her by the arm, collected her bag and began to walk her towards the door. "We're taking this somewhere else," I hissed.

Grace ripped her arm from my grasp. "No need for that. I'm going home," she said in a tone of voice that curled my toes.

Then she stopped. Turned around and focussed her attention on Seb.

He looked back and forth between the two of us and leaned back in his chair as if he was enjoying the show.

"Thank you for keeping me company this evening," Grace said to Seb.

"Not a problem," Seb replied, "I don't have as many commitments as my brother. I'm sure he would much rather have sat here with you all night." I made a mental note to thank him later for his much needed loyalty.

Grace turned her back on my brother and on me and marched towards the front door of the restaurant with me in hot pursuit.

With her years of training and ability to keep an eye on the entire floor, Mother must have seen the unfolding drama and managed to intercept the two of us before we'd made it half-way to the front door.

"Is everything alright?" She asked Grace the question and then eye-balled me. For some strange reason I felt like a fifteen-year-old who had screwed up his date for the senior ball.

"I'm not feeling terribly well," Grace said, "I'm sorry to leave so early, but I've had a wonderful time."

"Harry, please escort your date home, Seb and I can manage the rest of the evening."

"Honestly, there's no need," Grace said trying not to scowl at me.

"I insist," Mother said, placing her hand on Grace's arm. "It wouldn't be right for you to be out prowling the streets on your own at this time of night." She let Grace's arm go. "Now, off you go you two."

Having been given a leave of absence, Grace continued her march to the door.

Once we were outside, she stopped and turned on me. "There's no need for you to drive me home, I can walk from here."

I tried to make light of it. "You think that there's any chance I can defy my mother? You've worked for her."

Despite herself, the corners of Grace's mouth turned up into a semi-smile.

"She's a force of nature your mother."

"Come on," I said, let's get the car. I figured if I could get Grace out of here, I might have a chance to work out why she was so upset.

"Like I said, I can walk."

I watched in horror as Grace pulled off her high heels and began to walk down the track that I knew lead from the vineyard along the beachfront and down to Spindle Bay.

"I'm not letting you walk home by yourself."

Grace stopped and turned around to face me. In the dim light of the stars, I could see that she was pissed off with me.

"I don't need you following me home."

"You're either coming with me to get the car, or I'm following you. You're my responsibility for the evening and one way or another I'm going to make sure that I see you home safely."

"Fine," she said turning around and resuming her march along the track. Considering she was walking in bare feet, she set a cracking pace. "Do what you like. I've been walking these tracks all my life."

"You and me both," I growled after her.

She stopped again and I had to put my hands out to stop myself crashing into her body. As my hands found her shoulders to steady myself, I felt again that crackle of attraction between the two of us.

Grace sighed.

"Why do you want to ruin it all?"

"Ruin what?" I asked, as I pulled her body back into mine.

She allowed herself to lean her back into my chest. It had been a long and tiring evening for both of us.

"All of this," she sighed, waving her arms in a circular motion at the surrounding trees. We stood in an alcove of bush that lined the track. Shortly, these trees would give way to the tall pohutukawa below that reached for the bay and the sea beyond. The stars twinkled above us through the tree line. Aside from the laboured breath coming from Grace, I could hear the sound of the waves breaking on the rocks directly below us.

"If you put a wharf out from this headland, what do you think will happen to all of this?"

"Well, there'll be roading and earthworks."

Grace spun around, even in the subdued light I could see the passion blazing in her eyes. "And lights and people and concrete and street lights. Why? Why ruin a beautiful part of the Island?"

"Because we can't keep all this to ourselves, Grace."

"Well maybe I want to keep it all. Maybe I want to know that it's all going to be here, just the same, when I come back."

How had I forgotten that she was going away?

"Life moves on." Who was I trying to convince? Me or Grace?

"Well, I don't want to be a part of that moving on. I'm going to ask Kathryn for my job back on Monday."

I wasn't going to let that happen. "She won't give it to you. You're stuck with me."

"I can ask."

Grace turned away from me and started walking back down the path again.

"I saw the way your friend looked at you tonight," I said. Grace's step faltered. "You know that you can't go back to the restaurant."

"I don't want to talk about this anymore," she called over her shoulder speeding up. How she hadn't broken a toe or hurt her foot moving at pace in bare feet I didn't know.

"Okay, but I'm making sure that you get home." There was no way I was leaving Grace out here on her own at this time of night.

We walked the rest of the way to Spindle Bay in silence.

When we arrived at Grace's home I followed her to the front door.

She turned around to face me. "I'm home. You can leave now."

"This is when you're supposed to thank me for a wonderful evening and I kiss you goodnight."

"Kissing you tonight was a mistake," Grace said. "It's one that I won't be making again. Goodnight."

She put her key in the door walked inside and then went to close the door. Before she could close it, I said, "I'll see you on Monday."

The door slammed so hard I felt sure that it must have rattled the ancient timbers in the door frame.

Grace had spunk.

That was what I liked about her.

CHAPTER 14

*G*race

Chloe and I hadn't missed a Sunday brunch down at the Village since I'd returned full time to live on the Island.

Today was no exception.

I'd trudged my way down past the colourful painted boat sheds to our favourite mealtime haunt.

The Blue Lizard sat across the tar sealed road from Bounty Bay. All done in Retro furniture and up-cycled everything it oozed beachfront charm and nostalgia. It was nothing like the vineyard restaurant and I think that's why both Chloe and I liked eating here.

Jasmine sat over in the children's area with a number of other local children and a few who had come off the ferry this morning. They sprawled over bean bags in the early autumn sun and a few chased the ever-present seagulls and doves that came down for scraps from the cafe. No amount of *Do not feed the birds* signs stopped people from doing just that.

A chai latte sat steaming on the table in front of me. For

the first time since I could remember I nursed a small hangover. I still couldn't decide if it was because of the amount of champagne that I'd drunk, or because of the emotional turmoil that had kept me awake for most of the night.

Every time I closed my eyes, all I could see was Harry. I woke with my hand between my legs wishing that it was his. Why did I find him so overwhelmingly attractive when it had become apparent that he wanted to destroy the very things that I held dear about the Island?

My standard Sunday order of mushroom omelette with feta cheese and a green salad arrived by magic on the worn formica table. The scent of the food made my stomach roll, not unlike the roll of the waves from the beach across the road.

"Someone's looking a little green around the gills this morning," Chloe said as she tucked into a stack of pancakes with a grilled banana on top that swam in a sea of maple syrup. "Did you imbibe in one too many of the Pearson's best vintage?"

"I don't think so," I said as I gingerly pressed a tiny portion of the light and fluffy omelette to my lips.

"Well, something happened," Chloe said with an accompanying smirk plastered on her face.

"Mummy look," Jasmine arrived at our side, with a drawing of a starfish coloured in purple and pink.

"It's beautiful, darling," Chloe said admiring her daughter's artwork.

"You look sad, Aunty Grace," Jasmine said, "you can have it."

I stroked her dark hair. It was pulled high in a pony tail on the top of her head and a couple of bright coloured bobbles held it in place. "It's beautiful. I'll put it on my fridge."

She grinned, trapping the paper under my breakfast plate. "I'm going to do a shell next."

Then she was gone—back to the other kids and the contentment that came with the simplicity of colour and crayons.

I marvelled at the happiness that her intense focus brought her and longed for those carefree days.

I guess that's what upset me so much about what Harry had planned. I wanted this place to stay the same so that generations of kids could enjoy its unspoilt beauty—the way that Jasmine and the others were doing today.

"The festival went off without a hitch last night," Chloe said trying another approach to make me open up. I knew the tactic, it was one she'd learned off me.

"Stephanie hates me." I forced a button mushroom down and followed it with a sip of my latte.

"That bitch is just jealous," Chloe said putting down her knife and fork. She'd almost cleaned up her plate and I'd managed to get two tiny portions of my omelette and a mushroom down.

I took another sip of my chai latte and, for the first time since we'd sat down I let my eyes meet Chloe's and said, "Well, she's got nothing to be jealous about. Harry Pearson's an arsehole."

"You fucked him, right?"

I choked on my latte. "No!"

"Well, you're giving me nothing to work with here. What happened?"

I put the coffee down and resumed picking at my omelette. "I wish nothing had happened."

Chloe leaned in. "So *something did happen.*"

I couldn't help but smile. The memory of Harry on his knees in front of me refused to leave my head.

"You like him," Chloe taunted.

I let out a heavy sigh.

"But you wish you didn't."

She knew me far too well. "Something like that," I said nodding my head in agreement.

"So what's the problem?"

"What he wants to do with the Island and the vineyard. He's all about bringing the city over here and the idea of him destroying the beauty of a place like this kills me."

"But think about the work that he'll bring for people like me."

"I hadn't thought about it like that."

"You're leaving here," Chloe said, as she wiped up the last of her syrup with a wad of pancake, "The likes of me and Jassie this is all we've got. All we'll ever be able to aspire to having. Why not bring a few rich listers over here, it's got to be good for everyone?" Chloe put the last of her breakfast in her mouth. The action reminded me that I'd barely touched mine.

Was I being selfish? Only thinking about me and what I wanted in life? I'd always thought of myself as being generous. Maybe that wasn't the case.

"If that's the only thing that's standing in the way of you going for it with Mr Moneybags," Chloe said before putting her knife and fork down on her willow pattern plate, "then I say go for it."

"You would." If nothing else, Chloe's enthusiasm made me feel better about the situation.

"Did Stephanie bitch all night?" I couldn't resist asking the question. I needed to know what had gone on in the kitchen. It killed me being out the front with Harry, worrying about what people were saying.

"She whined like a wounded possum," Chloe's grin made me feel better, eased the tension I'd been carrying with me since last night. "You should have heard her complaining when Harry and Kathryn both gave her the evil eye."

"Kathryn too?"

Chloe nodded. "I know you've crossed some kind of mythical line." She held up her fingers and made speech marks over the last two words. "But who really gives a shit?"

I gave a shit. But talking to Chloe about it made me feel better than I'd felt since Stephanie had given me the first evil look. I knew I had to grow a thicker skin—but I wasn't good at dealing with the disapproval of other people.

Why you're hiding out here on the Island? The tiny voice in my head asked.

Sometimes I wished that I had Chloe's *fuck them all* attitude. Being with her, a little of it of it rubbed off, but not a lot.

"I saw Harry giving her a stern look, but I didn't realise that Kathryn was in on the act as well," I said.

"Yeah," Chloe couldn't keep the grin off her face. "If I was you and I'd gotten in with the Pearsons, I don't think I'd be sitting here on a Sunday morning moping about what a terrible life I had."

See there it was again. Chloe's ability to just step up on the attitude of those around her. Why couldn't I do that? Had the breakup with Nathan and the downhill trajectory of my life since then scarred me so much?

I shuddered.

The thought of the shame. Having to crawl to my parents. Leave what little of a life I'd made for myself over on the mainland and come here to lick my wounds.

I didn't want to make another mistake like that again.

Chloe might be suggesting that Harry Pearson was the best thing that had happened to me, but he also had the potential to be the biggest mistake I might ever make in my life. If I screwed things up here, there really would be nowhere to come back to and hide from the world.

I asked Chloe, "What would you be doing?" I tried to banish the negative thoughts from my mind and concentrate on what Chloe had to say. I also managed to get a couple of mouthfuls of omelette into my mouth.

Just sitting here with Chloe made me feel a hundred times better. The thought that I could screw up my life even further and never be able to come back to Hauraki Island and do this filled me with a sense of dread that I couldn't even name.

"Look," Chloe said, settling back in her chair. I had a feeling that she was going to give me another dose of *Life from Chloe's Perspective*. It was an interesting perspective simply because of the dreadful setbacks that she'd endured.

And she manages to stay here. To live in amongst it all a tiny voice in my head pointed out to me.

"You remember when Sam and me got together?"

"Who could forget that?" They were the talk of the Island. No-one gave them a chance of making it work.

He was from a poor Maori family in south Auckland. They worked hard. His mum and dad both had two jobs. He was the eldest of eight children. A good church going family, but they couldn't get ahead with the cost of rent and so many mouths to feed.

But, I did meet Sam's family. They had something special. They were a happy family. The tiny house was always full of whanau. Family visiting from down south.

They just arrived.

Sam's family did that on the Island.

They would show up without any notice. Stay for insane amounts of time and Sam never said anything about it. I didn't know how Chloe and her parents coped—but Chloe took it all in her stride because she loved Sam.

In summer, the Waters' lawn was full of tents.

They seemed to thrive on it. But the family had stopped coming since the accident.

"And you remember that no-one wanted anything to do with Sam at the outset?" Chloe asked.

"Yes." Where was she going with this?

"And did you see me worrying about what anyone thought?"

"No…"

"So why are you shitting on this amazing opportunity that's been put in front of you?"

"It's not about what other people think?" Who was I trying to kid? "I mean I was there last night because he paid me to be there. Double time."

Chloe just looked at me. She knew I was lying. I couldn't even lie to myself when she looked at me like that.

I screwed up my nose. "Does it sound that bad?"

"Aha," she said nodding her head. "You only have to look at the way you're moping around this morning to know that you like him. You can't let what happened with Nathan destroy your future." Chloe reached out and squeezed my forearm, "You just can't do that to yourself."

I started grasping for reasons not to get involved with Harry. "But I don't like what he's doing," I whined.

"Aren't you planning to go away?"

"Your point is?"

"You wasted so much time on that jerk at university."

"Don't remind me."

"So now you have a chance to enjoy yourself before you go away and look at you?" Chloe threw her arms wide, "Sitting here looking miserable. For fuck's sake. If I had the opportunity of someone like Harry Pearson even looking at me I'd be grabbing that sucker with both hands and never letting go."

Now I didn't know what to think.

Chloe carried on. "The one thing that Sam's death taught me is that life's short. You never know when your number's going to be up. Stop behaving like an idiot and get out there and have some fun."

Maybe Chloe was right.

Maybe I'd been worrying about what other people thought for far too long.

Maybe I needed to rethink my decision to go and see Kathryn on Monday morning and ask for my old job back.

CHAPTER 15

H**arry**

I'd attempted to throw myself into work on Sunday morning—but for some reason I couldn't concentrate. I needed to forget.

It had been a mistake bringing Grace back to the apartment. Why had I broken my own rule?

I couldn't look at the plans sitting on the dining table without seeing her lying there.

Open and willing for me.

Remembering the way that her face flushed when she came. The soft caress of her milky thighs against my face.

The taste of her.

I shook my head, poured myself another coffee and decided that I needed to make a plan.

Trying to work at the on-site office would be no better. Even a walk on the Island would bring her to mind. No matter where I went now all I could see was Grace.

I had an inkling of where this kind of thinking would take me. Straight back to Grace's doorstep.

Aside from the fact that I was a man who always got what

he wanted—I did have my dignity. She couldn't have been any clearer last night that she wanted me to piss off.

What I didn't understand was why she seemed so opposed to me creating work and a better economy for the people living here on Hauraki Island.

That's what my family had been about for generations.

First with forestry.

Then farming.

Now vineyards.

Without the Pearson influence, Hauraki Island would have gone the way of many of the provinces in this country.

Generations of unemployment and crime.

Is that what she wanted?

I finished my coffee and looked across the gulf to the city beyond.

Grace Richards wasn't going to tell me that we couldn't see each other. I didn't get where I was today without having to overcome a few obstacles.

Her resistance was just another obstacle to be overcome.

All I needed was a plan.

A plan that I could execute. I needed to show Grace that what I was doing was in the best interests of everyone concerned.

Hadn't I employed her to win over the locals?

If I couldn't win her over—what chance did I have with the rest of them?

I decided that I needed a swim.

There was something about the way the salt water ran across my body that helped me to clarify my thoughts.

The water was still temperate for this time of the year, but I pulled my wetsuit out of the garage. Long distance swimming meant that the buoyancy of the suit helped to hold me afloat.

The difficult task of peeling the suit up my body like a

second skin completed, I waded out into the clear blue water, then dived under.

A rush of cool surrounded my skin as the suit took on the thin layer of water that would act as insulation against the cooling action of the ocean.

I swam most days of the year. The only thing that varied with each swim was the thickness of the wetsuit.

Swimming always cleared my mind.

I made my way out to the 200 metre buoy in no time and then swung around to the left, so I swam just inside the 200 metre mark parallel with the beach. I'd been swimming the length of Spindle Bay since my teens.

I knew every current and nuance of the tide at every season. Over the years, I'd mapped every troublesome spot and every landmark as I swam.

Some of the landmarks had changed over the years and today as I swam the length of Spindle Bay I realised that me and my family were responsible for numerous of those changing landmarks.

The feeling didn't sit well with me.

As I reached the reef marker at the southern end of the Bay, I stopped for a few moments, treading water and looking back at the Island.

Where I'd entered the water, at the foot of the track that Grace and I had walked last night. That was where I planned to put the new wharf.

I could just see the speck of red that marked the old boat shed at the northern end of the beach.

Preliminary engineering plans that I'd looked at meant a new sea wall would have to go from the track, all the way around the northern tip of the headland. Large tracts of the sea bed would also have to be dredged and the spoil dumped.

I continued to tread water—enjoying the freedom and buoyancy. The muscles of my arms and legs had a warm tingle from the exertion of their movement through the water. Swimming this Bay each morning not only straightened out my mind, but it also kept my body fit and strong.

Would I still be able to swim the length of the Bay if we installed a wharf?

The logical side of my head said, yes. The emotional side of me wondered, probably the same way that Grace wondered, what would happen to the currents that I knew around this Bay?

The next logical step after creating a sea wall for a new wharf was to instal a marina. The island didn't have a large enough marina and the protected area of water that we created around a wharf would be the sensible place to instal a large marina. Another added attraction that would bring more people to the Island from the mainland.

As I continued to tread water, I thought about who these plans were really going to benefit. Were they in the best interests of the Island or were they about me putting my personal stamp on the Pearson empire?

The businessman in me suggested that I could quell Grace's fears by situating a new wharf and marina on the other side of the Island—but the preferred place for so many reasons was Spindle Bay.

As I set off on the return swim my mind began to clear. A plan began to formulate with each steady stroke through the water. I could find a way to have everything that I wanted.

But first, I had to get Grace Richards on side—and after last night, that was going to take all of my energy.

*G*race
Monday morning rolled around the way that Monday mornings always roll around. I'd gone to bed last night with less of a knot in my stomach. At least

after talking to Chloe on Sunday it had felt like less of a knot.

Now—this morning—the thought of facing Harry again in his office had me in a lather.

I was putting the finishing touches on my lipstick when there was a knock at the door.

A chill ran down my back. Surely he wouldn't come calling at this hour?

Relief swept through me when I saw the familiar red and yellow of a courier van through the trees.

A tiny parcel sat on the doorstep.

The only thing out of place on the perfect golden box with its matching golden ribbon was the shiny white courier label with my name and address.

Grace Richards
Spindle Bay
Hauraki Island

It still amused me. My family had been on the Island for such a long time that our surname and Spindle Bay was enough of an address for mail and packages to reach us.

Who could be sending me gifts? And on a Monday morning.

Harry a tiny voice in my head whispered.

That same voice that I'd been trying to ignore since Saturday night. It was getting more and more vocal.

And it appeared to be right.

I removed the lid of the package and the miniature gold card sitting atop yellow tissue paper caught my eye. I opened the embossed card. A single handwritten word in blue ink. I recognised the handwriting immediately, it said in a familiar and elegant hand, "Harry".

When I peeled the paper back, it revealed a single pair of yellow panties.

My entire body erupted in a swell of heat.

The vision of Harry with my panties to his nose came rushing back to me.

I swallowed, my throat suddenly dry.

My body ached all over again for the touch of his hands and mouth.

This had to stop.

But, clearly Harry wasn't going to make this easy for me.

My phone buzzed from over on the kitchen bench top.

A text from Harry.

"Do you have my gift?"

I thought about ignoring him, but that would be a silly thing to do. I was going to see him in less than half an hour for work.

The idea again of going and asking Kathryn for my job back in the restaurant flitted through my mind. Then I thought about the conversation I'd had with Chloe yesterday.

My fingers hesitated over the phone as I typed a single word response to Harry's question about whether or not I'd received his gift.

"Yes." I typed the word and then hesitated again before I hit send.

The screen flashed immediately as his response appeared.

"Wear them today."

My hands shook.

I wanted to tell him to fuck off, but something about those three words and the handwritten signature on the card called to me.

Harry had gone to quite some effort.

There was nowhere available on the Island to purchase anything like these panties. I could feel the weight of the material. The intricate design of the lace that edged the panties. These were not something that was knocked off in a sweat shop in China.

I didn't need to be a genius to see that Harry had gone to

some trouble to put this gift together. He'd actually been to a shop somewhere in the city. After a week in his office, I knew his handwriting. He'd taken a trip across the gulf and gone to the trouble of picking out underwear and writing a card.

The very card that I held in my hand right this minute had been in his.

I took a moment to think things through.

Everything inside of me wanted to rebel against the instruction that had come from Harry.

Then that tiny voice that I'd been trying to ignore—the one that wanted me to take a chance on him—the one that had been getting louder and louder screamed:

Go on. Live a little. Do It!

Did I dare?

CHAPTER 16

*G*race
I arrived at work.

Harry was already sitting at his desk.

The sight of him sitting there shook me more than I'd anticipated. I took a deep, calming breath and tried to behave as if nothing had happened between us on Saturday night.

I could do this.

I could be a professional.

"Good morning," I said trying to sound business-like. I felt anything less than business-like.

Harry looked up and all my promises to myself that I could be professional and that he'd have no effect on me whatsoever made a dash for the exit.

The way his eyes roamed over my body.

He looked hungry.

His face lit up when he saw me.

Dear god, I wanted him.

I didn't want to want him, but I seemed to have very little control over my feelings when I was around this man.

"How was your weekend?" he asked. His tone sounded

completely normal. How had he recovered himself so quickly from the way he first looked at me? It was as if he'd flicked some kind of switch in his head. Nothing about the way he looked at me now, or the tone of his voice when he asked suggested that we'd engaged in a mind-blowing sexual act at the weekend. Nor did it suggest in any way that he'd sent me an intimate gift of panties this morning.

But still, the constant undercurrent of attraction continued to sizzle between us. Or was I imagining it?

As I made my way across the threshold of the office door and to my desk, I pondered the evidence.

There was no getting away from the fact that, given another chance, we'd have searing and wonderful sex. Then I remembered that I hadn't actually answered Harry's question about my weekend. Something about being around him turned my head into a sieve.

"It was *interesting*," I replied and left it at that.

He let his guard down and the shutters came away from his eyes.

"*Interesting?*" He repeated the word and a prickle of heat ran through my body. He made it sound so dirty.

Then his mouth turned up into a smile. One that could easily have knocked the wind from my body.

Harry Pearson's smile should be outlawed.

I pulled out my chair and sat down at my desk. If I hadn't sat down, I could easily have fallen down—all the strength in my legs left me. The vision again of that face between them.

The same vision that had haunted my *"interesting weekend"*.

"I'm pleased to see that you haven't gone to see Kathryn and asked for your job back in the restaurant."

Fuck him.

He was teasing me and enjoying it too by the smirk on his

135

lips and the way his words danced across the distance between us.

"This one pays more." I said, pulling my skirt down across my thighs. For some reason the material had ridden up far too high as I sat down. Besides, I wasn't going to let him think that he'd persuaded me to come back here. I was my own woman and what he had to say wasn't going to sway how I carried on my life.

Yeah right, that tiny voice in my head said.

I told it to shut the fuck up.

A nod of Harry's head acknowledged my response.

Feeling in control, I turned my mind to the email program on my computer.

My traitorous head took a moment to think about the text Harry sent to me this morning and followed it up with another flash back of his head between my legs on Saturday night.

I clenched my knees together.

Fuck it.

What was I thinking?

How the hell was I going to work here with him?

You're out of options, my head took delight in reminding me.

"Leave whatever it is that you're doing," Harry ordered from across the room, "I've got plans for the day."

Plans! What kind of plans? My hands went sweaty and I looked back across the small room to see Harry closing the lid on his laptop.

"I'm clearing my mail," I said without looking back across the room. It seemed to be taking forever to open the program.

"I've cleared most of the email this morning," Harry replied, "the excavation team tell me that they're on track to meet their milestone at the end of the month, so I thought that you and I could work on our media strategy."

I looked back at him. Who was I kidding? I could spend hours just watching this man.

"Media strategy? After what I overheard at the Harvest Festival, I'm not sure that I'm the right person to be working on any kind of media strategy for you."

"You're perfect," Harry reassured me. Was he talking about my work skills or me? There were too many blurred lines here.

I was so out of my depth.

Again, I tried to put my personal feelings aside and focus on the business. "You know its going to take more than a media strategy to turn around Fish & Bird and their supporters once they hear what you have planned for Spindle Bay?" That was better. I needed to focus on the things that pissed me off about the Pearson operation. The words felt like bitter pebbles coming from my mouth. Anger gave me a sense of perspective—it had always given me a sense of perspective.

Harry stood up and I was reminded of the height of the man. Working with him in this confined environment was proving impossible.

I was an idiot.

"The conversation that you overheard," he said, "you know the wharf plans aren't set in stone yet?"

"Really? It sounded pretty set in stone to me." I pulled up the joint diary that I was managing for Harry. "In fact, I see that you've organised a meeting already with the Mayor's wife next week."

Harry waved a hand in the air. "Purely a PR exercise."

I couldn't help but raise my eyebrows.

"Don't look at me like that," Harry checked his phone. "I want you to come with me today. We're going to look at the entire Pearson operation. I want you to take some photographs. Do you have your camera?"

"No," I shook my head. "Why would I bring my camera to work?" I had a rush of blood to the head and all of a sudden I was feeling brazen. "If you wanted me to bring my camera to work, you could have asked me when you sent your text this morning?"

Did the colour of his face change or was I imagining things? Maybe I was imagining things but the fact that I'd put Harry on the back foot—even for a millisecond—was worth it. He stood with his mouth open, but no words were forthcoming.

Then, as if some part of his brain had re-engaged he said, "Are you wearing them?"

A neat recovery, but I wasn't about to let him off the hook. Not yet anyway.

"A lady doesn't tell," I replied, as I struggled to keep the best poker face I could under his intense scrutiny.

Taking control of the situation again, Harry said, "Come on." He made a move from behind his desk, but his movement must have been a little too quick. He sent his large, leather office chair careering into the back wall of the porti-com. The crash made me jump. Harry stopped in his tracks again. Checking out my reaction to the noise.

"You're not nervous about coming out with me all day touring the estate?" he asked one perfect brow arched.

"Of course not," I lied.

From the look on his face, he knew I was lying. But then I guess we were both playing a little short and fast with the truth at the moment.

"We should go," he said changing tack so fast I thought my head would spin and not a drop of alcohol had passed my lips this morning. "The four-wheel drive is out the back. I want to take you for a tour of the estate. Show you a few things."

"You're paying the wages," I said abandoning my computer and picking up my bag.

He looked at my shoes.

"You'll need some walking shoes. You can pick those up when we get your camera."

"Where are we going that three inch heels aren't called for?"

He tapped the side of his nose. "That's for me to know and for you to find out."

On our way out to the four-wheel drive, I decided that Harry might be right about the shoes. I realised as I stepped off the landscaped path that they were only good for office wear. I'd planned to walk home in bare feet, but there was no way that I could negotiate my way around the back of the porticom in bare feet.

It really did resemble a building site back here. It might be a short trip from the front verandah to where the four-wheel drive was parked, but along the way I had to negotiate a few interesting obstacles. Pieces of machinery, bright red scoria for drainage and a mound of soil and rubble lay in my path. It was clear that the rear of the building hadn't been landscaped with the same care as the front.

As I negotiated a tricky layer of sharp stones, I lost my footing and nearly went over on my ankle.

"Whoa, careful," Harry said. He had the foresight to collect me by the waist before I tipped too far over and prevented me from taking what could have been a nasty tumble onto my hip.

While he held me and helped my feet to re-establish sensible contact with the stony ground beneath them, I found myself staring into his blue eyes, my breath coming in tiny pants as the panic of nearly falling over subsided. With my body pressed against his hard chest and his arm wrapped tightly around my waist, all I could hear was the hammering of my heart.

He held me for far too long.

"Are you okay?" His eyes never left mine.

"I think so," the words sounded raspy and breathy—and far too sexy.

"Those shoes will never do," he said as he made sure that I was safely on my feet again. Not that I was in any kind of hurry for him to let me go.

The proximity of his body sent mine into a tailspin of desire.

I had to fight hard to resist the urge to lick him, he smelled so damn good.

You're at work the sensible voice in my head reminded me.

"Thank you," I said and I meant it, "I'll wear something more sensible in the future."

"You're welcome," Harry replied, "but you don't have to be sensible just for me."

Part of me wanted him to stop flirting. The other part glowed under the promise of his words.

Harry made sure that I climbed up into the four-wheel drive safely and then said, "The sooner we get you out of those shoes the better."

Shoes weren't the only thing that I wanted to get out of around Harry Pearson.

There was no doubt about it. I was in trouble and I think it was getting deeper by the moment.

CHAPTER 17

Harry

I gunned the motor on the four-wheel drive and we headed down to Grace's home.

It was the perfect time of year to show Grace the estate. I loved autumn. The harvest was in and the leaves on the vines were beginning to turn a delicate shade of yellow and red. The sun still warmed the earth, but there was the hint of a chill in the air in the morning and evening.

The long, hot dry days of summer were behind us and the entire earth had a feeling about it of looking forward to the long, dark days of winter.

I casually checked Grace as she sat beside me. The top was off the four-wheel drive and her hair which had been pulled back into a perfect bun on her head had slowly begun to escape in the breeze. Soft tendrils of straw-blonde hair framed her face. She'd put on a pair of large sunglasses that hid her expressive green eyes from my view.

I reminded myself that I had to take it slow if I wanted to make sure that my plan worked. But I didn't want to take it slow. Any more encounters like the last one getting Grace into the four-wheel drive would be the undoing of me.

Why were business transactions so much easier to navigate than personal relationships? I should have learned my lesson in Italy, but here I found myself, heading for naked and vulnerable with a woman who didn't realise how beautiful she was and what kind of effect that was having on me.

I wanted nothing more than to get Grace Richards in my bed. But I needed to take my time. I also needed to make sure that she understood my motives for what I was doing with the estate.

A day touring would be the best way to break down the wall that she seemed determined to construct between the two of us.

What I liked about Grace more than anything else was the way she stood up to me. It wasn't something that I'd encountered before. Most of the people I encountered in life wanted something from my family and they were willing to give something in return.

That wasn't the case with Grace.

She seemed determined to be her own woman and I admired that in her.

Grace came from a place of integrity that I'd not seen for quite some time. It made her even more attractive that she refused to bow down and accept that what I wanted to do would be in the best interests of the Island and those who lived here. I needed her to see that I had the best interests of the community at heart.

"Have you done any professional photography?" I asked as we neared the bach at Spindle Bay.

"Not really," Grace said.

"But the photographs on the wall, in your lounge, those are yours?"

"What makes you ask that?"

"They're pictures of Spindle Bay. Taken pretty much from your deck. You had a camera on the table when I called. I had to assume that they were yours."

"Yes, they're mine. Most people don't notice."

"You have a good eye."

I watched as Grace shuffled uncomfortably in her seat. She obviously wasn't used to being complimented on what she did.

"Thank you," she replied. "It's the reason that I want to go to Europe to study."

"But you went to university here in Auckland?"

"Yes," she nodded, "but me and commerce weren't a good mix. I don't like to talk about university."

That surprised me. Grace was smart. She should have excelled at university. "You didn't think about applying to art school?"

"Like I said, I don't like to talk about university." The tone of Grace's voice told me that I shouldn't try to pursue that line of discussion.

We travelled the balance of the short distance in silence.

I pulled up outside Grace's bach and went to get out of the four-wheel drive.

"Wait here," Grace said, "I'll change into something more suitable for traipsing around the vineyard. I won't be long."

"Okay," I said settling myself back in my seat. I'd love nothing more than to follow Ms Richards inside and help her change, but I wasn't going to argue with her.

Not right now, anyway.

*G*race

I stood in front of my wardrobe, wondering

143

what to put on. I decided on a simple orange and white dress with a sensible scoop neck and thin white over the shoulder straps. It buttoned down the front all the way through to the hem of the full skirt that finished just above my knees.

I put on a comfortable pair of brown hiking sandals, sensible shoes my mother had always called them. It was a shame I wore them for what felt like a situation that appeared to have nothing in the way of sensible going for it.

My mother.

What would my mother say about what I was doing now?

She'd tell me that I was playing with fire. More like an inferno sitting out there on the road in that four-wheel drive.

Mum would tell me to be sensible. To stay away from someone like Harry Pearson. The Pearson men were all bad news, she'd say. Look at the father and you'll have an idea of the son.

Well. Look where being sensible had gotten me.

Ticking all the boxes.

Miserable.

Spending time with a man I didn't love, doing a degree that could easily have driven me to suicide.

Chloe may have gotten the entire Island gossip machine going when she got together with Sam but she'd been deliriously happy.

Maybe I deserved a chance at deliriously happy. Even if Harry couldn't make me happy, he could make my last few weeks on the Island an awful lot of fun—especially if Saturday night was anything to go by.

At last! That persistent voice in my head said to me, *we're going to have some fun.*

I went to find my camera and realised that the cover was still sitting out on the table on the front deck.

I unlocked the glass doors and stepped outside to collect

the case. I was almost back inside when there was a resounding crack and I found myself leaning precariously on my left forearm. A screaming pain ran up my shin and I let out a yelp.

One of the old boards had given way under my weight. I put the camera case in front of me, grateful that it didn't hold the camera, the way it too had crashed to the ground. Moving my dress, I assessed the situation.

I had space to lean myself backwards and, with infinite care, I began to ease my aching leg out from between the broken plank of wood.

"What the hell, I told you that deck was rotten. Are you okay?" Harry was down on his haunches beside me in an instant.

"I thought I told you to wait in the car."

"Take it easy. Let me look at you." He went to move my dress and I slapped his hand away.

"Easy, tiger," he said, "I'm only trying to help."

"I know your kind of help."

"I'll behave, now let me get you out of there."

Clearly, he wasn't going to go away and leave me. I leaned back on my hands and realised that my arm hurt. I'd need to get some ice on it.

"You're pretty banged up," Harry said a note of irritation in his voice, "but I think I can lift you out without doing any more damage to your leg."

"It's only a scratch," I said ignoring the pulsing pains that were now running alternately between my arm and my leg.

With infinite care, Harry eased my leg and foot back through the gaping hole in the deck.

I looked down and my shin was full of blood.

"We best get you out to the doctor," Harry said eyeing the blood seeping out of the torn skin.

"Rubbish, it's just a scratch," I said. "We've a first aid kit in the bathroom. It's the big green plastic box underneath the basin. Can you go and get it for me?"

"Why don't I help you to the bathroom and you can show me where it is?"

"Okay."

"I told you that deck wasn't safe," Harry said as he slipped his arm around my waist and helped me to hop to the bathroom.

"Don't go on about it." I wasn't going to let him know, but I was pleased he'd come looking for me.

"It's nothing serious," I tried to reassure Harry, but he didn't look very reassured. "I can't tell you how many times one or another of us have fallen through that deck."

The look of mortification on Harry's face was almost worth being the latest victim of the dodgy deck work.

"You are joking?"

I shook my head. "No. The entire house has always been an ongoing project, you must have worked that out?"

"Clearly," Harry said, "and another reason that it's not safe for you to be here alone."

"Don't be silly," I said as with Harry's assistance I perched myself on the edge of the old claw foot bath.

"I haven't seen one of these in its original condition for years," Harry said taking in the chipped and stained enamel. "You don't bathe in here do you?"

Despite the pain in my leg I couldn't help but laugh. "No, the shower's tucked behind the door."

"Another renovation job that your family haven't quite got to yet?" Harry asked as he handed me the green first aid kit.

"Something like that." I popped the lid and found a bottle of disinfectant and handed it back to Harry. "Can you put a capful of this in the basin with some warm water, please?"

As he ran hot water into the basin and tipped in the disinfectant, the small room filled with the scent of pine.

"I really think we should be going to the doctor about this." Harry's concern touched me.

"We can make that decision once I've cleaned it up. Sometimes these kinds of things look far worse than they really are."

I drew in a sharp breath as I began to clean the now clotting blood from the front of my shin.

"It's not too bad," I reassured Harry. "Just a little scratch. See, it's stopped bleeding."

"You probably need a shot of something, the length of time that wood's been sitting out there."

"I had a tetanus shot not so long ago. I stood on a nail at the university campus." The memory of the way Nathan dealt with my injury that day and Harry's impeccable bedside manner couldn't have been more different.

"Okay, then. If you're sure you're okay. I don't want you collapsing on me or frothing at the mouth."

Chloe would probably say it was more a matter of me frothing at the mouth over Harry, but I wasn't about to share that thought with him.

"There's some tape and gauze in the kit, if you could pass it to me, please." There hadn't really been much damage at all. A long, ugly looking graze down the front of my shin. Keeping it covered for a couple of days should do the trick, I thought.

"Can I make you a coffee or something while you do that?"

"Tea would be nice," I replied, taking my time to measure out the right amount of gauze. "There's bags in the cupboard above the kettle and you can't miss the cups."

"On it," Harry said as he headed out of the bathroom.

Before he crossed the threshold into the small hallway he said, "Just call out if you need anything."

"I'll be fine," I replied. But I'd ended up in the one situation that I didn't want to end up in.

Alone in my home with Harry Pearson.

CHAPTER 18

*H*arry
        While the kettle boiled, I had a chance to take a good look around the bach. It was worse than I'd originally thought.

I'd already made the decision that I wasn't leaving Grace here on her own with a banged up leg and the house in such a state of disrepair.

From the lean on the floor in the bathroom, to the fresh air streaming in through windows that didn't close properly —there was enough here to keep one of my maintenance men busy for the rest of the winter.

No.

The place was a death-trap and there was no way I was going to leave Grace here while it was in this condition.

"Oh, good. You found everything," Grace said as she hobbled her way into the kitchen.

I took a good look at the front of her leg. I could see the reddened skin around the carefully placed gauze that Grace had taped in place.

"You should probably take some anti-inflammatories for the bruising. I didn't see any in the first aid kit."

"We can get some while we're out," Grace said as she sat down heavily on a chair that looked like it had been crafted by Noah. I worried about whether or not it would take her weight without crashing to the ground. I made a mental note to arrange for a new dining table and chairs to go on the list of things to be done.

I placed a cup of steaming tea on the white ring marked wood of the table in front of Grace.

"You can forget working today," I said as I sat down on the other side of the table, checking first that the chair would take my weight. "What I do want you to do is to pack a bag."

"What?" Grace almost spat out the mouthful of tea that she was drinking.

"You heard me," I wasn't going to take any kind of nonsense from her about this. "You've had a bad fall and I don't want you being here on your own—especially with the state the house is in. It's a death trap."

"It is not a death trap." Her voice went very quiet and then she said, "My family built this house from nothing."

"Come on, Grace," I struggled to contain my frustration at the state of the surrounding building. It should have been demolished years ago. Why her parents wouldn't accept our offer, I couldn't fathom. "How long really has it been since anyone's done any maintenance around here?"

Did her bottom lip tremble a little? I couldn't be sure. Grace looked up at me and then she shrugged her shoulders, almost in defeat. "I can't remember the last time Mum and Dad came to visit and my brother's overseas all the time. My sister," Grace rolled her eyes, "she's never been near the place since she married her husband." I let the words hang in the air between us. What should I say?

Then Grace looked around as if she was looking at the

property with a fresh set of eyes. "This bach belonged to my grandfather and he passed it down to my mother. I guess one day I'll inherit it." Then she set her eyes on me. "Unless, of course, mum makes the decision to sell it to someone like you who will put a bulldozer through it."

"Look," I said, holding my palms up in defeat and trying not to sound like an arsehole, "Maybe we can compromise." Grace continued to eye me suspiciously. "At least come and stay with me for a couple of nights. I'll have one of our maintenance guys come down here and take a look. Make the place safe for you to stay, so at least I won't have to worry about you falling through the floor and crippling yourself."

She shook her head. "No. It's not your problem." I could tell by the determined set of her jaw that she wasn't going to make this easy for me. "Besides, I'm going away in a few weeks and then it won't be an issue at all."

This was a ridiculous argument to be having. "Look. I'm not having you come back here and fall through another board on that deck. At least let me get the rotten boards replaced, some decent locks on the doors and the windows fixed so that they close."

Grace stood firm. Shook her head. "No. I can ring Dad and get him to come up and fix the boards."

I was losing patience. I tried to sweeten the deal, "You don't need to bother your father. We have all the equipment needed up at the vineyard. Let's call it payment for the photography that you're going to do for me."

Grace tipped her head to the side, considering my latest offer. "If you put it that way then," I could see she was on the verge of accepting and a strange sense of relief began to flood my body. Grace nodded her confirmation. "Okay."

"Good, I'm glad that's settled," I said taking a drink of my tea. "Now just get your bag packed and we'll be out of here."

"I draw the line at coming to stay with you."

I eyed Grace over the top of my chipped tea cup. "I have a guest suite. You'll be left alone." Was that a flicker of disappointment I saw cross her features? "Unless of course, you don't want to be left alone."

Grace dropped her eyes to her tea.

She felt it too.

The inextricable push and pull of desire that had been playing between the two of us from the moment that I'd picked her up off the floor in the vineyard restaurant.

*G*race

I'd given up trying to fight with him.

Harry Pearson was a man who got what he wanted.

Something about that excited me. Maybe it was because I had a sense that he wanted me.

I packed my bag, almost grateful that someone wanted to take care of me. My leg had begun to throb and the idea of staying in the bach on my own while I felt like crap didn't appeal at all.

Now I sat in the four-wheel drive on my way back to Harry's apartment.

I'd arrived at the vineyard so many times since I'd taken a job here, but lately every time the lines of the vines came into view, with the panorama of the ocean behind them, it had been as if I was seeing the entire estate with a new set of eyes.

It seemed that I'd been looking at a few things in my life lately with a new set of eyes.

We pulled down the driveway of the Pearson homestead and out around the back to Harry's wing of the house. Out of nowhere, I found myself sitting in a pool of anxiety.

Why had I said I would come here?

I should have held firm. Insisted that I stay at the bach.

You want him. The tiny voice in the back of my head whispered.

That was why I'd agreed to come here today.

"How's the leg?" Harry asked as we pulled to a stop and he turned off the engine.

"I think I'll live," I replied. "Shouldn't you get back to work or something?" If I was going to get acquainted with Harry's apartment, I'd prefer it if he wasn't actually here.

"I was planning to show you around the estate, if you recall, before you fell through your deck."

Harry got out of the vehicle and came around to the passenger side to help me out. I winced as my foot hit the ground, residual pain radiating up my shin from the scrape.

"I have some anti-inflammatories inside. We'll get those into you and you'll feel better."

It did feel good to be looked after. "I'm being a baby. I'm sure we could still go out and take a look at the estate."

"That can wait until tomorrow," he said as he let us both into what was now the familiar foyer of his apartment.

"The guest suite is down here," he said as he walked past the staircase that we'd climbed at the weekend. Was it only a day ago? It seemed as if so much was happening in such a short timeframe.

"You'll have everything you need here," Harry said as he put my bag down on a double bed large enough to sleep four people. "The bathroom is through here," he said pointing to the right where I could see a white, tiled room not unlike the one I'd visited upstairs. "And this is one of my favourite rooms in the wing," Harry said as he took my hand and walked me through to a spacious sitting room. It seemed like the most natural thing to do, to stand there with my hand in his, admiring the view out across the small paved terrace to the vines and the sea beyond.

"Now," he said, as he turned my body to face him, "I want you to make yourself at home. Treat the apartment like your own. Everything you need should be in the bathroom and there's a cupboard full of food upstairs."

I felt as if I'd been transported to some kind of alternate universe.

Harry stroked a tendril of my hair away from my face. "You know I want you, Grace," my heart hammered in my chest as his fingers ran down the side of my face and then paused at my chin. "But I'm not the kind of man who's going to force myself on you."

Why not? That traitorous voice in my head screamed.

"When you decide that you've gotten over whatever it was that upset you on Saturday night," I went to say something but he pressed his fingers up against my lips. "Hear me out."

I nodded my acceptance and he removed his finger. I wanted him to touch me again.

"When you decide that you want to talk about Saturday night, let me know."

"Okay," I whispered.

"Good," he said. His voice washed over me. The sound caressed me, held me rooted to this one spot.

"You sit down and get comfortable and I'll go and find some of those tablets."

For a reason that I couldn't fathom and probably for the first time in my life, I simply did as I was told.

I settled myself down on an overstuffed sofa that had a bright yellow and green floral pattern to the thick material. In any other setting it would have looked out of place, but here, by the edge of the doors that lead out to the paved terrace and the gardens beyond, it fit.

The gardens that I looked out at comprised clipped box hedges and topiary that looked as if it had been growing here for decades. The gardeners did such a good job, I could easily have believed that the clipped hedges didn't dare push a single leaf out of place. A sigh escaped my lips. The lush greenery had the effect of creating a tranquil oasis.

Beyond the formal plantings I could see the edge of an orchard, the familiar branches of plum, pear and apple trees marching off into the distance before they met the formal lines of the vineyards that dominated the view.

I could understand why Harry enjoyed sitting here. Unlike the view from the room upstairs, you could feel a real connection to the land in this space.

"Right," Harry said as he returned with the promised painkillers. The packet sat on a tray, with a jug of juice, a tumbler and a boysenberry muffin. "Make sure you eat this, so the tablets don't upset your stomach."

He'd thought of everything.

"Thank you. But honestly, I'm okay to go back to work."

"How about you have something to eat and drink and then we assess that position after the tablets have done their thing?"

"All right." It was clear that he wasn't going to let me go back to work.

"Here," he said, pushing an ottoman towards me that was covered in the same bright material as the chair that I sat in, "put your foot up on this."

I did as I was told without complaint. I could begin to enjoy being looked after like this. I couldn't remember an instance in the whole time that Nathan and I were together that he'd ever cared for me this way.

"I'll be upstairs in my office if you need me," Harry said with a nod of his head and then he was gone.

CHAPTER 19

*G*race
    After I'd taken some tablets and eaten the
    muffin, I felt much better.

The stinging from my shin had begun to subside. Now there seemed little reason to sit here. I wanted Harry to show me around the vineyard—falling through the deck had caused all manner of trouble.

Like the house—so much of the inner workings of the estate were not made available to the public. It wasn't as if wine-making were some kind of secret, but I guess the family decided to take care with who they let in to see their particular methods.

To be allowed to tour the estate, especially with Harry Pearson as my guide, well why wouldn't I want to take up that kind of opportunity.

The thought that Harry still wanted to upgrade the estate's facilities and generate more traffic to our Island weighed on my mind. Maybe, after I'd taken a look at the rest of the operation, I'd have some more of an understanding of why he felt the necessity to improve things.

I'd also be in a better position to inform Fish & Bird about what was going on. My allegiance felt split. Harry was paying my wages, but I'd done so much photography for Fish & Bird and I cared so much about the Island. My loyalty to the Island would always win any kind of argument in my head. I resolved to keep Fish & Bird in the loop unless ordered otherwise by Harry.

Besides, I told myself, Harry had been clear that there was no kind of gag order imposed on me. Then I recalled his mention of the word, "trust" on Saturday night and something inside of my gut rolled over.

What loyalty did I really have to the Pearson family?

It was one of the reasons that I didn't want one of Harry's maintenance men down at the bach making repairs.

Chloe would ask me what was I worrying about?

Hadn't I been on the payroll two days ago when I'd lay across the table upstairs for him? The thought of our encounter upstairs should have disturbed me—instead, it excited me.

Harry had said that he wouldn't touch me unless I wanted him to.

The question I really had to ask myself was what did I want?

Until I answered that question—all the others would pale into insignificance.

It would be so much easier to cut and run. Book my flight and forget that Harry Pearson ever existed.

"Enough!" I said out loud. Getting to my feet. If I sat down here any longer thinking through the entire situation, I'd go mad. I needed to be out doing something, not sitting here like some kind of caged bird wondering whether or not to go upstairs and ask Harry Pearson to fuck me.

There.

An honest thought at last.

That's what I wanted.

I went and found my camera, turned it over in my hands and then thought about taking a couple of shots of the sitting room. I decided that wasn't a good idea. A good idea was getting out of this house.

I guess the only sensible thing to do at this stage was to go and look around the estate with Harry. I'd rested my leg long enough that I was no longer limping. In fact, I was certain I was well enough to be going back to the bach tonight—but I couldn't imagine having that argument with Harry again.

I put the camera back in its case and went looking for Harry.

The walk upstairs wasn't quite a replay of my visit on Saturday night, but the way I was feeling, it may as well have been. I was acutely aware of the fact that I wore the panties that Harry had delivered this morning. As I walked into the main living area of the apartment, my bare feet padding across the warm wood of the floor, my memories of Saturday night had turned me into a ball of sensual anxiety.

Harry leaned in the open doorway between the living area and the deck with his back to me. Even from this profile, his entire body oozed control and sexuality. The sight of him pushed my body temperature to boiling.

I could hear the beat of my heart thrumming it's accompaniment to every step I took towards him.

I stopped half-way between the table and the deck. Took a deep breath and then said, "Hi."

Harry turned in a lazy fashion towards me. He had a cup of coffee in his hand. "I was enjoying the view," he said, "but I think this one's even better."

A shot of heat flared from deep inside of me, radiating its way out toward my chest and my face.

"How are you feeling?"

"Much better," I said trying to get my temperature under

control, but likely failing to do so. "I thought we should go out and take some of the shots that we'd talked about this morning."

Harrys eyes raked across my body before dropping to the scrapes on my leg. "You sure you're okay to be going out?"

"Honestly, it's a tiny scratch. We should get on and I really should go home tonight."

If I came back here tonight, it was pretty obvious to me that I was going to end up in Harry's bed.

"Okay," he said and a swell of relief flooded through me. "We'll go and take a look around the vineyard, but I'm not letting you go home until I'm happy that the house is secure and safe."

Why wasn't I surprised that he wouldn't back down? I guess we had something in common—other than our seething attraction to each other—we were both stubborn and wilful.

"I'll get my camera and meet you outside in five minutes," I said trying to at least find some way to take control of the out-of-control situation I found myself in.

"I like a woman who's happy to take the lead," Harry said. "I'll see you downstairs shortly."

I had to wonder again what kind of lead Harry was talking about.

Truth be told, I think we both knew that he wasn't talking about whether or not I met him at the car.

*H*arry
        It felt good.

Having Grace sat beside me as we made our way around the estate. I'd taken her through the vineyard's grape crushing facility, and onto the large storage sheds where we housed the maturing wines in oak barrels.

"These will all be going underground into the caves that we're constructing," I said. "It's a constant issue for us managing the temperatures in these vast warehouses and, putting the barrels underground will keep them at a much more even temperature."

Grace nodded her understanding and continued to take photographs of the lines of oak barrels that filled the vast space.

"What will you do with these spaces when you have storage underground?" she asked.

I knew it was a leading question and it was one that I was tempted to try to avoid. But something about the way that Grace looked at me, I was compelled to tell the truth. "I've been looking at plans for turning the entire space into apartments. But-"

She cut me off, "You know that they say everything post the but is bullshit don't you?"

I couldn't help but laugh and was rewarded by a surprising smile from Grace.

"If you'll hear me out?"

"Okay," she said, resting the camera on the strap around her neck and leaning on one of the large barrels.

"This is likely not a sensible place to put apartments. I don't know that people would enjoy living so close to the operational area of the vineyard and moving the entire processing facility may well not be an option."

"Okay," Grace said, "but you're still not off the hook. I haven't forgotten your plans for a piazza."

I was quite sure that she hadn't.

"Come on," I said, "we're going to lose the light and I want to show you one of my favourite places on the estate."

It didn't take us long to get from the processing plant to the top of one of my most loved paddocks of vines.

Grace had busied herself taking photographs of the views

and the vines themselves. I loved them at this time of the year—post harvest the leaves were changing and the roses that sat at the head of each row of vines were still in full bloom.

With the heat of the sun on my back, I almost felt as if I could relax. For the first time since I could remember, I even felt like playing hooky and taking the rest of the afternoon off.

I loved watching Grace work. She had such a passion for photography and it had become more apparent to me the longer we'd been out together how much she loved what she was doing today.

"It's probably better to be out taking photographs at this time of the day," she explained as she stood in the middle of the upper vineyard. "With the sun so high in the sky, we're not going to get too many shadows across the lines of the vines. We'll get better definition on the finished photographs."

I could happily have sat here all day and watched her point that camera. It must be interesting to see life through a lens.

"What do you want these for?" Grace asked as she came back to the four-wheel drive. I'd been sitting on the hood, enjoying not only the view out to the Gulf, but also the sight of Grace. If it were possible, she came more alive with a camera in her hand.

"You know you were wasted on commerce. I can tell just by watching you how much you love your art."

Grace shrugged.

"The camera has been an extension of me for as long as I can remember."

"All the photographs in your bach, did you take them?"

She nodded. "Yes. They've gotten better over the years." She swiped a stray tendril of hair away from her face. I was tempted to follow her fingers with my own, but then I remembered that I'd promised her that any relationship had to be on her terms not on mine.

That was some kind of concession from me. I usually took what I wanted when I wanted it. But with Grace. For the first time, I wanted her to come to me, and I wanted her to come to me for the right reasons.

"The latest photos I've taken for Fish & Bird they're the best photographs I think I've ever taken."

No wonder she was opposed to me putting a wharf in at Spindle Bay if she'd been doing work for Fish & Bird.

"What were you doing for those communists?"

Grace's head swung around. "They're not communists. Just because they care about the environment."

"Man," I said, "you bite faster than the fish around here."

She scowled at me. "You shouldn't joke about things like that."

"Things like what?"

"People who want to keep an eye out for the environment and the creatures that live in and around our coastline."

"You're implying people who keep them safe from hungry commercial operations like mine?"

"Something like that," she said putting the lens cap back on her camera and stowing it in the case.

The entire mood of the moment had changed. The warmth that I'd felt from the sun dissipated with the criticism from Grace. A lot of people had criticised me in the past and I didn't care. Why did I care so much about what Grace thought of me?

"You do know that I care about the environment, don't you?" For a reason that I couldn't fathom, I was compelled to try to defend myself.

Grace leaned against the bonnet of the four-wheel drive, close enough that I could catch the sweet scent of her body.

"It's hard to believe with your family's track record for destroying native habitat."

"Turning green fields into vineyards is hardly destroying native habitat." I'd stood on many fields as a child and watched the seasonal workers put in posts and rails and dig planting holes to put in vines. The vines that produced grapes up here were nearly as old as me.

I'd spent hours as a teenager trimming and tying these vines. I had an investment in hours of labour in many of these fields.

Grace turned and looked me square in the eyes. "Your father burned off the entire headland north of Spindle Bay to put in acres of vineyards. Would you like me to take you back to the bach and show you the photographs of how that headland looked before he set to stripping and burning it off?"

I had no idea what she was talking about. "It was green fields. I watched them plant the vines."

"Before he turned it into vineyards. Didn't your family graze cattle and sheep on your land?"

"Well, yes." I thought about the paddocks. "All I remember is green paddocks. Dad never burnt off any land. I'm sure I'd remember something like that. I recall removing the last of the cattle runs. We used the wood for bonfires on Guy Fawkes. But you can't accuse me of abusing the environment. Hell, I swim down in Spindle Bay every morning."

Grace's face softened.

"I know you swim. I've watched you from our deck. I can swim out to the buoy, but I can't imagine doing the lengths of the Bay that I've watched you do."

She's watched me swimming. Something about that sentence intrigued me.

"Spying on me, Miss Richards?"

The colour around the base of Grace's throat changed.

"I'm a photographer," she reminded me, waving her

camera in front of my face. "I also happen to know the breed of every dog that walks the beach of an evening as well. What kind of photographer would I be if I didn't notice what's happening in my environment?"

"A very bad one, who might have to be punished."

Grace's eyes went wide.

"Well, I guess if I don't want to be punished," she cast her eyes to the ground, "we need to get on." Then looking back up at me, she added with a smile, "I'm sure you have other things you'd like to show me?"

Boy did I have things I wanted to show Grace—but in her time—not in mine. We both knew we were going to take this to another level of intimacy. It was just a matter of when.

Grace would come to me because I always got what I wanted.

And it would be sooner rather than later.

CHAPTER 20

*G*race
    Harry had been the perfect gentleman all day. Why did I find myself wondering what he was up to?

No doubt, because the mutual feeling of attraction continued to swim between us. Despite our differing opinions on his plans for the Island, he'd not tried to coerce me into anything I didn't want to do. Well, did insisting that I stay at his apartment instead of going home count?

I wasn't sure anymore. Given the choice now, I'd happily agree to staying, but in any event, he'd gone out of his way all day to treat me with nothing but respect.

The longer I spent around this man, the more I realised that I'd fallen hard. I didn't want to admit it, even to myself, but the thought of leaving Harry behind to go to Europe had begun to hurt.

Especially after the delivery that arrived this morning—I had a sense that Harry sent a pair of panties because we both knew that he would likely be removing them tonight.

My body shuddered.

"Cold?" Harry asked with an amused look on his face. He opened the front door to his apartment and stood aside waiting for me to pass in front of him.

"I'm fine," I replied.

He slipped his hand into the small of my back and ushered me inside. "I didn't get a chance to tell you this morning with everything that went on how beautiful you look."

"In these old things," I tried to brush off the compliment, but Harry wasn't having any of it.

"Those old things look stunning on you," he purred as he slipped his lips over mine.

The unexpected kiss—like everything else about Harry these days—ratcheted my nerves up to intolerable. When Harry pulled away, leaving me feeling bereft and alone he said, "I'm looking forward to seeing if you're wearing the gift I sent you this morning."

A shot of heat ran through my body and then he pressed his lips to mine again.

This time I was almost ready for him.

My hands of their own volition found their way to his neck. My fingers slipped into his thick, dark hair.

Tired of trying to do the right thing and tired of fighting the attraction, I surrendered to Harry Pearson.

"Come," he said when our lips finally parted for the second time. "I'll get some dinner ordered for us. You can rest up that leg."

"You mean you don't cook?" I couldn't help the little dig as I followed Harry up the familiar stairs.

"I can," he said over his shoulder, "but I prefer to make use of the restaurant facilities. Or we could go down and have dinner with my mother in the dining room of the main house."

Holy shit! No! My head screamed.

"Order away," I said as I sat down on the familiar Starck couch in front of the picture window. I could see why the Pearson family had located their home on the top of the rise. "You must never tire of this view," I said staring out as the shadows began their lengthening dance into the evening.

"It's the main thing that I missed while I was away," he replied while he dialled the number for the restaurant. "The view and my daily swims at Spindle Bay."

"They'll be compromised if you put in a wharf at the northern end of the beach," I said.

Why are you trying to piss him off? That small, insistent voice in my head screamed. *Let it go.*

But for some reason I just couldn't.

Harry didn't have a chance to respond. He ordered dinner for us both and by the time he got back to the couch where I sat with a bottle of wine and two glasses in hand, he'd either decided to ignore the comment, or let it go.

I watched him pour the wine and I still felt as if I'd walked into an upmarket hotel suite. The large open plan room, like the rest of Harry's apartment, was impeccably presented, not unlike its occupant.

"This is nice," I said, digging around to find a way to fill the silence between us. "I do understand why you were drawn back to Hauraki Island." Harry sat and studied me, not saying a word. We both knew why I was here and that it was just a matter of time before I would be in his arms.

"Yet, you're still insistent that you have to go overseas to study," Harry said eventually breaking the silence. He leaned back against the couch and casually crossed his legs. He seemed so at ease with himself and the situation.

I on the other hand, like I had been for most of the day, was hyper aware of the presence of his body. Every movement he made affected me somehow as if a giant force field shifted between the two of us.

He stood up and I jumped. "I'll set the table, dinner will be here soon."

I watched with fascination as Harry moved, not unlike one of the staff who worked in the restaurant, with infinite care to lay the table. Fine, white bone china and delicate crystal soon adorned the surface.

"I should probably get out of these clothes," as said as I stood up and made to go downstairs.

"You sure you don't want me to help?" Harry asked.

"Maybe later," I replied trying to sound as casual as possible as I walked past him heading for the stairs.

He caught my hand and pulled me back against the hard length of his body, his arm encircling my waist.

"Don't play me too long, Grace," he growled.

"Surely you want to take a shower before dinner?" I asked. "We've been traipsing around the vineyard all day."

His eyes never left mine.

The heat of mutual desire played between us.

"You've got ten minutes before dinner arrives," he said, "and make sure you keep that leg dry."

"My leg is perfectly fine," I replied.

The rest of me though, I couldn't be too sure about.

*B*y the time I returned, Harry was sat at the table waiting for me. His dark hair, damp from his own shower had taken on the deep black of a Tui's wing.

He pulled out a chair for me and then popped the cork on a bottle of the estate's vintage champagne. He poured us both a glass of the bubbling liquid and then sat down across the table from me.

"A toast," he said holding his fluted glass aloft.

"To what?"

He eyed me, his eyes filled with the heat of the lust that

sat between the two of us. "To you. To Spindle Bay and to the fascinating future that lies ahead."

I replied, "To my planned trip to Europe and the experiences that await me."

Did I see a slight frown cross Harry's face? If I did, he recovered his composure as we touched glasses.

As I took a sip of the amber liquid, the bubbles tickled my nose.

"You're determined to leave the Island then?" Harry asked as he began to remove the silver lids from the serving trays that the food had arrived in. A sumptuous fragrance filled the air.

"That's the plan," I replied, trying to sound light-hearted about it.

"I ordered fish of the day, with baby roast vegetables and romesco sauce," Harry said as he began to serve. "Well, I have to warn you, Grace," Harry said as he placed the food on my plate, "I'm going to do my very best to persuade you to remain on Hauraki Island."

There.

He'd said it.

Not only setting the food out on the table, but setting out his intentions.

I spent the next twenty minutes pushing my dinner around my plate. I'd eaten barely anything. The sumptuous food had been lost on me. My overarching anxiety playing havoc with my senses because I could feel my own need to be touched by Harry. He'd been nothing but the perfect host and that wasn't what I wanted.

My body ached to be caressed by him.

I had a yearning need that I wanted him to fulfil for me.

I knew he was seducing me. Drawing me in little by little and I could see from the look on his handsome face that he was enjoying the game.

"Come, Grace," he said and stood up from the table. Harry held my chair for me as I stood up and indicated with the wave of his hand that we should move to the leather couches on the other side of the room. "I want you to sit down and make yourself comfortable." My body no longer shook with anxiety. The champagne and the food that I had eaten had settled my nerves.

"You know I want you, Grace," Harry said as he took a seat next to me.

Heat rushed to my face and I could feel the flames of it spreading down toward my chest. "Do you want me?"

"Yes," I answered. It didn't seem worth even trying to hide my desire. Harry had sensed it anyway.

"Good," he soothed, his voice even and his tone soft as caramel, "I want you too. Did you like the underwear I bought for you?"

I nodded.

"I thought it only fair that I should buy you a new set, since I've still got yours from the last time we saw each other."

The reminder of Harry walking away with my panties in his hand turned me on.

"Pull your dress up and show me what the new pair looks like."

I moved my hand and then hesitated.

"You have a beautiful body, Grace," Harry said, "I want to see it. Now show it to me."

Under Harry's intense gaze and with shaking hands, I reached for the hem of my dress and began to pull the material towards my waist. By the time the cool evening air reached the top of my thighs I could feel myself getting wet.

"Good girl," he said. "You take orders so very well."

I took a deep breath as I pulled my skirt the rest of the way up my legs and exposed myself to Harry.

"Now," he said, his voice still reflecting the total control he had over me and the situation. "I want you to slip your hand inside of those panties I bought for you and touch yourself."

By this time, the combination of my desire for Harry and my newfound ability to do as he commanded had made my movements slow and languid. In fact, I discovered that I liked having him look at me. Harry made me feel desirable and powerful in a way that no-one had ever done before.

The feeling was more intoxicating than the champagne that we'd drunk with our meal.

I did as I was told and slipped my hand inside my swollen wet folds. I closed my eyes and imagined what Harry was seeing. I could smell my own arousal.

I jumped and opened my eyes as his hand surrounded my throat. The unexpected confining touch made me moan.

"That's it, baby," he said, "slip a finger inside yourself."

I did as I was asked.

"You wish that was me, don't you?" he growled, his face only inches from my own. The scent of Harry surrounded me—musk and feral heat.

"Yes," I whispered as his hand slid down my chest, pushing the thin straps and material of my dress down to my waist and liberating my lace covered breasts.

"So beautiful," Harry moaned as his lips followed the path of his hands.

I dropped my head back on the cool leather and sucked in a breath as Harry's fingers found my nipples. They pearled under his touch as he circled them through the fine lace.

"You want me to pinch them, don't you?"

My body shuddered at the thought of the delicious pain travelling through me.

"Yes," I said.

"Say please."

"Please," I whispered. As the word left my lips, the shock of the pain travelled from my breasts through my body to my core. I don't know what excited me more—the pain or the fact that Harry made me tell him to do it.

I arched my body into his and let out a long moan.

"Yes baby," he said. "I want you to keep moving those fingers in and out of yourself. I want you to think about my hard cock being in there, but don't you dare push yourself over the edge. That's going to be what I do to you tonight. But I want you to think how it's going to feel when I'm sliding myself in and out of you and you're screaming my name as you come."

It wasn't so much the way Harry said the words, or the words that he used that turned me on. It was the fact that I had total control. He wasn't forcing me to do anything that I didn't want to do and yet I knew I was powerless to refuse what he asked of me.

"I want to come," I moaned.

"Not yet, baby girl," Harry said as he covered my hand with his own so I couldn't move it anymore. "Come on," he said as he picked me up off the couch and carried me out of the room.

CHAPTER 21

*H*arry
    I was never going to let this delicious woman out of my sight. After I'd spent the day with her, watching her come alive photographing the vineyard—I knew she was the one.

The one for whom I would do anything and everything. And now I was going to claim her. Mark her as my own.

I sat Grace on the side of my large bed and then relieved her of the burden of her clothing. Her skin quivered under the touch of my hands. Her body, heated and ready for me.

The sight of her naked was nearly enough to push me over the edge. One touch of her body and I'd be gone.

I took a deep breath.

Worked to regain my control.

I wanted to make this last.

It felt as if I'd been waiting for Grace all of my life, not just since I'd helped her up off the floor in the restaurant. But still, I needed to make the moment last. To savour the anticipation and drive Grace to a tumultuous orgasm—the memory of which would never ever leave her.

I kicked off my shoes and socks and said, "Undress me."

The sultry smile that crossed Grace's features told me that she'd been waiting for this moment with exactly the same anticipation as I had been. Her breasts swayed in a lazy motion as she moved off the bed towards me and I smelled the sweet scent of roses that I'd come to associate with Grace. I had the overwhelming desire to push her back on the bed and climb on top of her, but instead, I waited patiently for her to begin undressing me.

Tonight, I knew that this would be the beginning of something beautiful. The beginning of the relationship that I'd waited all my life to find. To think, that I'd found my Grace here, on Hauraki Island.

This Island had given me everything and now it had given me my Grace and I was going to do whatever it took to keep her here with me.

Grace

Taking instruction from Harry seemed like the easiest thing in the world to do.

I started with his shirt, pulling it off over his head. It was as if Harry had given me himself as a Christmas present.

As Harry leaned forward and allowed me to take the soft piece of clothing from his body, the tapestry of ink that I'd first spied under the tail of his shirt became apparent. Almost one entire side of his upper body and a large portion of his lower back was clothed in an amazing, colourful portrait.

I stopped and simply stared.

"You're shocked," Harry said.

"No," I shook my head taking in the swirls of blue and red ink interspersed with images of vines. It was as if he carried the imprint of the Island across one side of his body. "It's amazing," I breathed as I reached out and began to trace the edges of the images, where colour met his natural skin tone.

"How long did this take?"

Harry watched me in the intense way that I'd become accustomed to his eyes following me. His skin flickered under my touch.

"Many months," he said. "I had it done while I was away. I took pictures of the landscapes to artists. This is an Italian's interpretation of our Island."

The way he said *our Island*. The words had the sound of coming home about them.

The rest of Harry's body didn't disappoint—it was the polar opposite of my own soft flesh. A wall of hard, defined muscle moved under my fingertips. I couldn't keep my hands away from him and as I ran them over the warmth of Harry's skin and ink, I was rewarded by the sound of soft moans coming from him.

"You're beautiful," I said as he remained unmoving and in total control.

"Don't stop," he said as my hands came to rest in amongst the light hair that covered his chest. His eyes continued to watch my every move.

I took hold of the buckle on his thick leather belt and wrestled the strap through the heavy metal before pulling it from his jeans.

Harry's erection made it difficult to undo his jeans and I couldn't help but smile.

"Look what you're doing to me," he said and I didn't have to look far once I'd gotten the button down fly undone.

He sucked in a long breath as my hand encased his thick cock through the thin material of his underwear. I couldn't wait any longer to see him completely naked.

With a push of my hands, Harry's underwear and jeans slipped down his legs and he stepped out of them.

I found myself face-to-face with a thick, upright cock.

"Suck me," Harry growled.

The hunger in his voice turned me on and I slipped my lips over the smooth, silken head of his cock. The guttural moans that came from above me were nearly my undoing.

My heart beat faster. I could feel the pace of my own arousal increasing as I bobbed and sucked Harry's thick, hard cock.

The sense of power and control that swept through me turned me on more than anything had ever turned me on before. To have this influential man—a man who could silence an entire room simply by walking into it—at my mercy and moaning as a result of my touch, filled me with an indescribable feeling of heat and desire.

"I can't stand any more," Harry gasped as he took a hold of my head and pulled me off him. "I want inside of you, where I've wanted almost from the first time I saw you."

Before I knew what had happened, he slipped a condom over his cock and had me spread eagle in front of him on the bed.

"Are you sure this is what you want, Grace?" he asked me with a degree of self-control that I'd never seen from anyone.

"Yes," I breathed. I wanted him inside of me. I'd been on the cusp of coming almost from the moment that we'd sat down to dinner this evening. The touch of Harry's cock at the mouth of my wet lips was almost enough to push me over the edge.

"What do you want me to do, Grace?" Harry asked.

"Fuck me," I heard myself say.

Harry rolled over onto his back and said, "Well, you take me then. You fuck me until you can't fuck me anymore."

I wasn't waiting for another invitation. I climbed atop this virile, carnal creature and slid his cock inside. I gasped as he filled me.

Harry's eyes were wild with lust. His hands came up and cupped my breasts. "You're so very beautiful and you're mine," he growled as he thrust himself deep inside of me.

I rode him.

I threw my head back and I languished in the pleasure of taking this powerful man.

The pleasure of release rolled through me.

Harry groaned from under me. Pumping his hips high and then settling under me—surrendering to his own release.

Afterwards, he pulled me to him.

Slipped his arm around my waist and held on tight.

"You're beautiful and you're mine," he murmured into my neck as our bodies settled around each other.

We fit.

My last thoughts were that Harry had given me something tonight that no-one had ever given me before—and given it to me in so many ways.

The chance to be me.

The chance to experience an awakening of a sexual power that I hadn't even known lived within me.

I adored him.

I loved him.

I always wanted to be with him.

But how could this ever work?

I woke early, just as the sun began to rise. I could hear the familiar sound of the gulls on the foreshore making their morning calls.

The orange glow of the rising sun filled the large room.

I padded across the floor, collecting my clothes from in amongst Harry's where they'd been thrown last night.

Harry had woken me at some time in the middle of the night and made slow, sensual love to me.

Last night had been perfect. It was a night that I'd never forget. I'd carry it with me forever.

I looked back at him. Asleep. I wished I had my camera with me to capture the image, but I knew it was one that I wouldn't ever forget.

As quietly as I could, I padded in bare feet down the stairs to the guest suite below Harry's living quarters.

I felt blessed that I hadn't packed much to bring here. I could be out the door and on my way home before he even woke up.

What I felt for him was too terrifying.

If I didn't leave now—I may never leave and there was so much of the world out there that I had to experience.

As I turned to make my way back out of the living room Harry leaned in the doorway.

"Going somewhere?" he asked. He wore nothing more than a pair of cotton boxer shorts.

I swallowed. "I need to get home."

"You know I don't want you to go?" Harry slipped his hand against my face, his fingers, slipping around my ear. I couldn't help but tip my head sideways into the cup of his hand.

I was powerless in the presence of this man.

"I have things to do." I'd find something to do. But I needed to get away from here. Think things through. Unscramble the thoughts that ran through my head. I couldn't think straight while Harry was around.

"I'd like you to stay." The sound of his voice rolled over me. Reminding me of how it felt when his hands roamed my body.

I looked up into his clear blue eyes. "I know." It took every inch of my willpower to resist touching him.

"But I won't keep you here against your will." Harry dropped his hand to his side, releasing me from his touch.

Could he read my mind?

I almost wanted to laugh.

No.

Harry didn't need to read my mind. I had my bag in my hand. It wouldn't take much to put two-and-two together and work out that I was leaving.

"I'm not running away."

He cocked an eyebrow, "Are you sure?"

I wasn't sure. I hadn't been sure about anything since the moment I allowed myself to be carried to Harry's bed.

My eyes found their way to the window and fell on the lines of the formal garden. "I wasn't making things up when I said last night that I needed to leave the Island." Why couldn't I look at him when I said that?

Harry slipped a hand either side of my face and turned my eyes so I looked directly at him. His touch was like more than coming home. It felt like an anchor, or a magnetic field.

It held me.

Drew me to this Island.

Something about the way I felt when Harry Pearson touched me terrified and excited me all at once.

"I understand your need to explore the world outside New Zealand," Harry ducked down to my height, lowered his face to below my eyes. Looked up at me as if he were pressing home his point. "I really do."

What could I say in return?

I made an attempt to walk past him, but the bulk of Harry's body prevented me from walking through the door frame. He didn't move.

"Well then you'll understand why I have to get away from here, too," I said. I felt like I was drowning.

My frustration mounted because I couldn't get away, I threw my hand in a circle above my head. "None of this is real. You live in a fantasy world. One that I can't be a part of. That was so obvious to me the night of the harvest festival."

"You belong here the same way that I belong here," Harry said, his voice soft. Understanding.

"If you leave, the gulf will call you back. There's no getting around that—it's what happened to me. You don't think that Europe isn't somewhere that a man with grapes in his heart shouldn't live?"

Not only in his heart, I thought. The image of the vineyard lay in beautiful colour all over his body.

But he'd been away and come back. I hadn't even been away.

Harry ran his thumb down my cheek.

Despite myself, I wanted to take that thumb in my mouth —instead I tipped my head again into the hollow of his hand and allowed the warmth of his palm to calm my frayed nerves.

"We're the same you and I," Harry whispered as his lips touched the skin where his thumb had just been.

"We love this Island and the people who live here."

He nuzzled the scruff of his unshaven face against the skin of my own.

I shivered.

It was as if I was in a perpetual state of movement every time Harry was anywhere near me.

"But I still need to go," I said looking up into his eyes. Willing him to take his hands from my body and let me pass.

"You do," he said with a heavy sigh. "I understand. But promise me one thing, Grace," he said as he let me go and stood aside allowing me to pass.

"What's that?" I knew I shouldn't ask, but I couldn't help myself. In so many ways I was helpless in the hands of Harry Pearson.

"Promise me that you'll come back."

I walked away—I couldn't make that promise.

I wasn't ready to make that promise.

The silence hung heavy in my wake.

"Grace!" Harry called after me.

I turned to face him.

"Let me drive you home." He looked down toward the healing scrape on my leg. "Your leg."

I couldn't help but laugh and the corner of his mouth turned up.

"What?" He asked.

"You got me here on the basis that I was crippled after falling through that deck."

At least he had the temerity to blush—I could see the colour climbing his face even from the other side of the room. It gave him a sense of vulnerability that tore at my heart. If I didn't leave now, I'd never leave.

If I wasn't so determined to make my way off this Island, I could easily have crossed the room and fallen back into his arms. Into his bed and permanently into his life.

"You can't blame a guy for using every opportunity to his advantage."

I shook my head. "No, I don't blame you for anything, Harry. But I'm quite capable of walking the track home. You and I both know it's only going to take me less than ten minutes."

I turned and walked out the front door of Harry's apartment. I hesitated as I closed the door. Had I just shut the door on the best thing that would ever happen to me?

For me, it was now or never. I knew that much.

CHAPTER 22

*H*arry

I watched Grace leave the room.

There was a sense of purpose to her stride.

There had always been a sense of purpose about Grace—another reason I ticked off in my head that I liked her.

It took me a few moments to realise that I should have insisted I drive her home. But then—I smiled to myself—this was Grace Richards we were talking about. I remembered the way that she stubbornly walked home after the harvest festival. What would ever make me think that she'd allow me to take her home?

Independent and proud.

My mother.

She reminded me so much of my mother.

The only other woman in the world that I loved.

Then it hit me.

I rushed up the stairs. If I was fast enough, I might still catch her. As I flung the doors to the deck open, I realised I was too late. Grace had already passed the end of our formal gardens and disappeared into the folds of the bush and pohutukawa trees.

But, I had a plan.

I checked the photographs that we'd downloaded to my computer from the photo shoot yesterday, along with a whole raft of shots of Spindle Bay that had been on Grace's camera. I sent an assortment of them to the printer in my office and then brought them back out to the dining table.

The dishes from last night's dinner were still laid out on the table.

I pushed them to one side and laid out the printouts of the shots Grace had taken. Some I'd blown up and I began to rearrange them on the surface like some kind of crazy, abstract jigsaw puzzle.

One of the pictures she'd taken on the top vineyard caught my eye. There was something about the way that she'd managed to get the light between the lines of the vines. A subtle shift that someone who hadn't grown up around the Island wouldn't have seen.

The same warm feeling that I'd experienced that after-noon, sitting on the bonnet of the four-wheel-drive. The feeling that I didn't care. That I could let work go and just be. I was filled with that feeling again.

Contentment.

Was that it?

I couldn't just allow that contentment to walk out of my life and hope it came back.

One of the dawn shots of Spindle Bay that had been on the camera as well caught my eye. The glorious vignettes that she'd managed to catch. The reflection of the light upon the water and the clever placement of vegetation in the shots.

I wanted to keep Grace here on Hauraki Island—but she wanted to study overseas. Why didn't she study here?

"Why hadn't I thought of this before? An idea hit me like a freight train.

I grabbed my laptop from under the small mountain of prints and selected a few of the shots that I loved.

I emailed one of the gallery owners that I knew in town. From what I could see, these were far too good to only be used in advertising material for the vineyard.

Grace had a talent.

She'd been wasted on commerce there was no doubt about that in my mind now that I'd seen the final shots that she'd produced.

I dialled Frederick's number.

"Harry, how are you?" the familiar voice of my friend boomed down the line.

"Fred, I'm good."

"I enjoyed the Festival at the weekend."

"It was good to see you, man."

Not much for pleasantries, I got right to the point. "Are you in front of your email?"

"Yes," he replied.

"You should have one from me, with some photographs from the Island and the vineyard."

"Hang on a minute." It seemed like an age I waited. How long could it take for a few photographs to get to town?

"They're here," Frederick eventually replied.

"What do you think?"

"They're fantastic," he exclaimed. "Where'd you get them? The light and the colour are especially appealing."

"A girl we have working for us."

"She's got a real feel for lighting and composition."

"You think so?" I thought I was simply smitten with everything about Grace, it was nice to have some kind of confirmation from someone else.

THE PACIFIC BILLIONAIRE VINTNER

"I know so. I could easily put some of these in the gallery and get good money for them."

This was pretty much all I needed to know. "Do you still have any contacts at Art school?"

"Plenty. Why, does the photographer want to study?"

"She might." Those seeds of an idea were well and truly beginning to germinate.

"You know I'm always looking for new material for the gallery. Do you think your lady might like to exhibit some of this work?"

I owned the work. I'd effectively paid Grace for it by having the maintenance done on her family bach. I didn't need her consent.

"She'd love to."

"Great," Frederick said. "I'll have my PA email some details of suitable dates."

"Earlier the better," I replied. I wanted to get Grace's work up in a gallery as soon as I could.

If the frame of mind she'd just left here in was any indication, I didn't think it would be long before she was getting on a boat and not coming back to the Island.

I'd always had the ability to make things come together at speed, but I needed this to come together fast.

"Your contacts at the Art School?"

"Yes," Fred replied.

"Can you get your PA to send me those details as well? I'll say I've come with a recommendation from you, if that's okay?"

"I'm always happy to help out the Pearson family in any way I can," Fred said.

Great. This was coming together and in a better way than I could ever have hoped.

"I'll make sure that we send a crate of our best vintage to you for your trouble."

"There's no need," Fred said.

"No, I insist." One good deed always deserved another and Fred had made it possible for me to see a way of keeping Grace here on the Island. That alone was worth a hell of a lot more to me than a single crate of our best vintage.

A hell of a lot more.

Grace

As much as the wonderful times I'd had with Harry kept swimming through my head, I knew that I'd been living some kind of fantasy.

True to his word, the windows in the bach all now closed properly. The deck had been patched and my new front door key shone like a bright star on my key ring. How was I going to explain the changes to mum and dad? I pondered whether or not I should make sure I was out of the country before I sent them an email—but I guessed that would be the coward's way out.

I wasn't a coward.

That was why I'd just booked my flights.

It had been a surprise, checking my bank account and finding an extra $2,000 with the words *BONUS4PRINTS* on the screen. I'd talk to Harry about it. It wasn't necessary—especially after the work that he'd done around the property.

What did cross my mind was that with the extra money Harry had given me for the shots I'd done around the vineyard I had plenty in my bank account to keep me in food and lodgings in Europe.

I'd get a seasonal waitressing job as soon as I could and get my life back on an even keel.

No more trying to ignore men like Harry Pearson.

No more having to worry about the changes he'd like to make to the Island.

No more wondering whether or not I had the courage to go.

The flights were booked and I'd be out of here in two weeks.

I'd funnelled enough information to Forest & Bird for them to make submissions to the council and make sure that the correct legal channels were followed.

I simply couldn't stand aside and watch Harry and his family destroy Spindle Bay—no matter how much money he thought it would bring to the Island.

There was too much at stake. Too many people who would be affected. There had to be a way for everyone to compromise. I wasn't opposed to the developments and the improvements he was making to the vineyard, but I couldn't sit around and watch the entire Bay—a Bay that had been such a huge part of my life and the life of my family before me—be destroyed.

I opened my email program and found Harry's email address.

It was time to write my formal resignation.

A single line would do it.

It seemed strange, writing such a formal letter to him—especially after the intimate night we'd shared in his apartment—but I knew it was the right thing to do.

The wrong thing to do would be to check out without giving him two weeks' notice.

I guess all I had to do now was make it through the next two weeks with Harry.

What would Chloe tell me to do?

I picked up my phone and dialled her number.

"Hey, how's it going?" The sound of her voice gave me some comfort.

"I've just resigned and I've booked my flights. I'm out of here in two weeks."

"What about Mr lover boy boss?"

Could she hear the quaver in my voice? "I guess I've got two weeks to enjoy him, or stay away from him before I go."

"You guys done the deed yet?" Chloe had a way of making something that had been so beautiful sound so seedy and dirty. My inclination was to say no. It seemed that I didn't need to say anything.

"Your hesitation to answer's all I need to know," she said. I could hear the laughter in her voice.

"Was he good?"

Now I felt the heat of a blush as it exploded on my face. I twirled the tea cup on the table next to my computer. It occurred to me that it was the cup that Harry had been drinking out of the other morning. Why did everything around here now remind me of him?

"I'm not even going to answer that question," I replied. Talking about Harry with someone else seemed so disrespectful.

"That good, huh?" Then she added, "Better get your fill before you go."

The idea of being with Harry again and then leaving… I didn't know if I could go there. "If I go near him again like that, I don't think I'll be able to get on the plane."

This time the line fell silent while Chloe thought about what I'd said.

"Maybe if that's how you feel," she replied, "you shouldn't have booked those flights."

"You're supposed to make me feel better," I whined.

"What do you want me to say? 'Great. Go for it. Leave behind everything you love-'"

"Who said anything about love?" The L-word terrified me. Love meant giving up what you wanted. Putting yourself last. Putting your dreams on hold to follow someone else's dreams. I'd already tried that. It didn't work.

Chloe laughed. "You wouldn't be ringing me if you were happy about what you'd done." Then she added, "And maybe you do love him. Have you thought about that?"

I'd thought about nothing but Harry. It was doing my head in. I thought that booking my flights and sending my notice might have been the best thing to do.

"I've given my notice," I said trying to defend myself.

"Has he responded?"

"Hang on, I'll check."

I opened my email. Nothing. I knew that Harry received his email direct to his phone. He dealt with every email as it came in.

"No," I said. "Strange. He normally deals with everything as soon as it comes in."

"Maybe he's not going to accept it," Chloe suggested.

"Well, he's going to be in trouble in two weeks when I leave and he's got no-one there to assist him," I said. I knew I sounded more confident than I felt.

"You never know with the Pearson family. They've always got another agenda running." And with that interesting thought running through my head, Chloe said, "Gotta go. The kid's let the kindy rabbits out and the dog's on the loose."

The line went dead and I was left wondering what, if any, alternate agenda Harry Pearson might be running.

Then I saw him.

He hadn't replied because he hadn't seen my resignation.

The lone figure that I'd watched for so many years swimming out to the 200 metre buoy—on his way to do his lengths of the Bay.

CHAPTER 23

*H*arry
I'd returned from my morning swim and the first thing I'd read was Grace's resignation.

Fuck!

I wouldn't acknowledge receipt. I wasn't about to let her think that I was okay with her leaving. Not after last night.

She'd booked her flights.

Fuck!

There was no way I was going to let her go. I had to make her see that staying here with me was the better option.

I'd left a message with the Dean of the Art School, but I'd had no response. I contemplated ringing again, but then had a better idea.

But first I needed something to eat.

There was nothing in the apartment, so I headed down to the family kitchen.

"Ah, you've surfaced." Mother met me with a knowing smile.

I kissed her on the cheeks, "You can take that look off your face," I said.

"You and Miss Richards driven from your apartment looking for food." The jest was in good humour, so I let it go. My mother had no knowledge that Grace had just resigned and I wasn't about to let that sour what should have been a jovial morning exchange with another woman who loved me.

Did Grace love me?

The question in my mind irritated me.

I knew she felt the connection between us. There was no doubt in my mind that Grace was running. Running from something that should have terrified me too.

But I wasn't going to let her go so easily.

It had taken me a long time to find someone like Grace and now that I'd found her—losing her again wasn't an option.

"Grace has gone home," I said forcing myself to sound casual, as I made a bowl of muesli and fruit and availed myself of one of the French pastries that mother always had on hand in the kitchen. "Coffee?" I asked her as I threw a cup under the espresso machine and punched in a particularly strong capsule of coffee.

"I'm fine, thank you," she replied. Mother was dressed in her regulation jeans and t-shirt. Ready for another Tuesday at the restaurant.

"What are your plans for the day?" she asked.

"I'm going over to town. I have an appointment with Frederick at the gallery. He's going to show some of Grace's portraits of the vineyard." And he was going to be showing them in the next week. If I had to arrange for a hundred boxes of our finest wines to be delivered to him.

"Portraits?" Mother looked confused. "I didn't know that Grace was a painter?"

"Photography," I said between mouthfuls of breakfast.

"I commissioned her to do some work for the marketing

material I'm putting together around the development and it seems that she has a much better eye than I'd originally anticipated. According to Frederick."

Mother tipped her head to one side. "Well, if Frederick thinks she has an eye—she must be good."

"Exactly."

"So what's in this for you?" Mother asked.

She always had an uncanny knack of getting right to the core of the issue. That's why she'd been so successful. The reason the two of us had managed to navigate our way back from the abyss that my father's drinking and womanising had created.

"Why does there have to be anything in it for me?" I'd at least try to play coy. It's something that mother and I had enjoyed for many years. An elaborate dance of ideas. It had helped us find our way to the root of many a problem over the last few years. We formulated a strategy and then stream-lined that strategy to get us where we needed to be.

"Harry, you really think that I haven't forgotten that Grace is leaving us very soon. I do believe that it was you yourself who told me she planned to hand in her notice and go overseas."

"I should have kept my mouth shut."

"So you do want her to stay?"

"Possibly."

Now mother laughed. "I don't think I've ever seen you watch a woman the way you watched Grace on Saturday night."

An uncomfortable creep of heat ran up my back.

"That doesn't mean a thing," I replied, taking a bite of the sweet pastry and enjoying the sensation of it melting in my mouth.

"I also saw the way that Grace watched you. Even with

Seb sat at her side her full attention was on you for the entire evening."

"That must have pissed him off." I couldn't help laughing and mother joined me.

"Indeed," she agreed. "I am blessed with four extremely attractive sons, but the media would have us believe that Seb is the most attractive of the four of you."

"That may be so," I countered, "but it has to be said that your three older sons are far less trouble put together than your youngest."

Mother rolled her eyes, "Don't we know it. But you can stop trying to change the subject."

I looked at her, my expression blank.

"You've told me more than I needed to know. I am your mother, remember and I do recall what it's like to be in love."

There was that L-word again.

For some reason it didn't phase me to hear it.

"Look," I said scanning the room to make sure that Seb was nowhere to be seen.

"Your brother was out on the town last night," Mother said leaning in a little closer to me, "he won't be up for at least another two hours, whatever you have to say will stay between you and me."

So much of what I'd said over the years had stayed between the two of us. That was why the business had begun to flourish under our joint control.

"Yes," I'd finally admitted it to another soul. "I want Grace to stay and I have a plan."

*M*y plans complete from my visit with Frederick and a productive couple of hours with the Dean of the Art School, I slowed the boat as I approached the beach in front of *Ridgedale*. Deploying the wheels of the amphibian watercraft, I waited for the familiar bump as the three of them connected with the firm sand of the Bay.

As the boat began to rise from the sea, I killed the prop and lifted the motor from the water.

The amphibian craft trundled up the beach and into the red boat shed that belonged to *Ridgedale* and had sat at the northern tip of Spindle Bay for as long as I could remember.

I had a sudden flashback.

Standing with my grandfather as a child. Playing in the sand of the Bay and watching him as he painted the doors of the shed. I remembered the smell of the paint, stepping around trays and brushes covered in layers of colour. The scent of the solvent that he soaked the brushes in.

A fleeting, but painful thought ran through my head. If I was to build the wharf along this edge of the Bay as planned, then this iconic boat shed, along with a vast portion of the rock pools and splash zone that I'd walked with my grandfather as a child would go.

The entire area would disappear under a sea wall.

I could almost feel the weight of the wrath of my grandfather on my shoulders as I parked the amphibian craft in the old shed. I shut down the motor and sat there and thought about what I wanted to do. The whole of the shoreline would be dredged and the entire end of the Bay reshaped if my plans went ahead.

You've been around Grace for far too long. I said to myself.

But, as I vacated the boat shed and began to secure the old, red doors I couldn't get the idea out of my mind. As I pulled down the familiar wooden board that had served as a secure lock for multiple decades—I couldn't help but think about one of the beautiful photographs that Grace had taken of this very spot.

Progress. I reminded myself. Progress and opportunity didn't come without some kind of change.

I was all about change and that was what I'd been negotiating today.

There were three parts to the plan that I had begun to put in place.

Operation Saving Grace, my mother had named it.

After the negotiations that I'd been in this afternoon—it felt more like *Operation Saving Harry.*

Maybe it was the start of something that would save us both.

I looked back at the red roof of the boat shed.

A shiver ran down my spine. It was almost as if the familiar hand of my grandfather had touched me.

"It's just the wind," I said to myself. I was getting far too sentimental. This wasn't like me at all. I had no attachment to anything. I'd worked hard since my father had screwed this family over to ensure that never again would I feel the loss of anything.

If it hadn't been for the foresight of my grandfather who had put Ridgedale into a trust that my Dad couldn't gamble away who knew where we'd have all ended up. Homeless, and penniless no doubt.

No.

Grace Richards wasn't going to derail my plans for the vineyard.

But she may well have made me think again about the possibilities for the waterfront.

As I walked the familiar path back up to Ridgedale from Spindle Bay, I had a new appreciation for the little wax eyes and fantails that flitted between the branches of the pohutukawa trees. The wildlife were filling themselves up on the last of the summer harvest and putting down a layer of fat for the winter.

What would become of these little creatures if this area was cleared to make way for a road down to a wharf on the headland?

These were questions that I hadn't thought about before. Grace had forced me to look at things from a different perspective.

I wasn't about compromise in any way, shape or form. But maybe for this woman I could rethink my plans.

First, there was the matter of making sure that everything was in place for tomorrow.

I could scarcely wait for Grace to come to work.

race

Wednesday. I'd always called it 'hump day'.

Harry hadn't come to the portacom at all yesterday. The only time I'd seen him since I left Ridgedale had been for his morning swim at the beach.

I met this morning with a special kind of dread. Would he be here today? Or maybe he was working from his office in his apartment, like yesterday.

It had been nearly twenty-four hours since I'd sent Harry my resignation and I'd received no acknowledgment whatsoever.

I walked the track up to the portacom with trepidation.

Sel, the foreman who was looking after the construction of the wine caves acknowledged my presence with a tip of his head.

It was a shame, I thought—that I'd miss the opening of the cellars and the eventual building of the piazza. I still held firm to my hope that Fish & Bird would put an end to the idea that a wharf at the tip of Spindle Bay would be built to service the development.

I took a deep breath and stepped inside Harry's office.

There he sat.

As he'd always sat until the night of the Harvest Festival.

A sudden vision of him lying in his bed assaulted me. The way he held his arm above his head. The fall of the rising sun across the light feathering of dark hair on his chest. The sculptured shape of his strong shoulders. Shoulders that propelled the rest of his muscular body through the salt water of Spindle Bay.

"Good morning," Harry's eyes didn't leave his computer screen as I crossed the threshold.

"Good morning," I replied, the words the only competing sound as my heels clicked their way across the small space to my desk.

I opened my email, hoping against all hope that there would be some kind of acknowledgment from Harry of the resignation that I'd sent to him.

I scanned the mail.

Eventually my eyes fell upon a line with Harry's name.

Thank god for that, the tiny voice in my head said as I clicked on the email. But it wasn't what I was expecting.

I read the contents and then looked up.

Harry was eyeing me with intense what? Curiosity?

I flicked my gaze back to the email and re-read the contents.

This couldn't be happening.

Then I rechecked the list of incoming mail—just to make sure that I hadn't missed another email from him.

Nothing.

"Well?" Harry said from the other side of the room, "Are you going to say anything?"

I didn't know what to say. Instead, I stood up and made my way to the coffee machine. I learned a long time ago that if I didn't know what to do, I should do nothing.

"Coffee?" I asked as I pushed an extra strength coffee capsule into the machine. Harry had it installed when he worked out that the coffee habit we shared may well have come close to competing with the national debt.

"You should know me well enough by now," Harry replied, his tone showing no emotion.

I know you far too well, my head said.

"I take it that's a yes?"

"Is there a problem with my communication?" he asked.

He knew damn well that there was a problem with his communication.

"You haven't acknowledged my resignation," I said concentrating on the hot liquid pouring itself into the red coffee cup in front of me.

"I'm not going to acknowledge it until after the exhibition."

My stomach lurched.

"You didn't mention anything about putting my photographs in an exhibition."

In my mind's eye I could see the invitation that Harry had emailed to me this morning. What favours had he pulled in to get one of the most prestigious galleries in Auckland to put on a show of my work—and at such short notice?

"Frederick liked them. I can't understand why you've never shown any of your work. He seems to think that you've got talent."

I placed a steaming cup of coffee in front of Harry and then retreated to my own desk. I may not be able to put much space between the two of us, but I'd do my damned best, at least while we were at work.

"I've booked my plane tickets."

"They can be cancelled," he said in a dismissive tone.

I don't know what I expected to see on Harry's face, but

the words didn't elicit any kind of emotional reaction from him.

"They're non-refundable."

That did elicit a reaction.

He smiled at me and then took a sip of his coffee. Something inside of me hummed, despite my best intentions, I had no defence to this man's charms. "Money's not the issue here, Grace," he said as he placed the cup with care back on the saucer on his desk.

Then he crossed the short distance from his desk to mine.

With a shaking hand, I took a sip of my own coffee and held the cup in front of me, as if somehow the cup and its contents could magically protect me from the force that was Harry Pearson.

"Money's never been an issue for me," Harry said as he perched himself on the edge of my desk.

My temperature soared and it had nothing to do with the cup of coffee in my hand.

Harry continued to stare at me, his eyes full of passion. "I've worked damned hard to make sure that I get what I want," he said as he leaned in towards me.

I could hear the sound of my heart beating as he took the cup out of my hand and placed it with equal care on the saucer on my desk. "And I want you." I felt the words as they brushed my face, "here with me."

His lips were so close I could smell the fresh coffee on his breath.

"Permanently." He whispered the last word as his lips slipped over mine.

"*I*s there any reason we can't get the ferry like normal people?" I asked as Harry helped me up into the bow of the amphibian that resided in the red boat shed at the tip of Spindle Bay.

"I've never done anything like a normal person," he said as he climbed up beside me and sat down in front of the steering wheel.

It was useless trying to argue with a Pearson when they'd set their mind to something. After our kiss, it was also clear that Harry and I were going to get no work done until I at least bowed to his wishes and went to see the installation for the show.

"You didn't think to ask me whether or not I was happy with having my work shown?" I asked as Harry backed the boat out of the shed and set us on our way. It seemed strange, to be sitting in a boat and travelling across the sand to the water's edge.

"You wouldn't have let me." He smiled as the boat hit the water and suddenly we were floating.

Harry edged the motor down to half-way and we began to pull out to the 200 metre buoy at a gentle five knots.

"I'm pleased to see that you keep to the speed limit inside the marker buoys," I said.

"You forget," he replied with a grin, "I swim out here. I've had the odd close call with an idiot who doesn't know or respect the rules."

How could I forget that Harry Pearson swam the beach?

Once we were past the large yellow marker buoy, Harry fully lowered the motor and gunned the engines. The wind whipped over the front windscreen and there was little chance for conversation as we cut across the gulf.

We were pulling into the wharf at Auckland in less than half the time it would have taken had we come by ferry.

Harry manoeuvred the boat into a small berth at the Marina and then took my hand to help me disembark.

Parked not far away was an Audi, not dissimilar to the one he had on the Island, only this time with a nice hard top.

He ushered me inside the vehicle and I found myself in the middle of Auckland, heading for upmarket Parnell.

Frederick's gallery was positioned at the top of the rise and Harry parked the car no more than a couple of feet from the door. No doubt more long-standing family ties meant the two families had been working together for longer than I had been alive.

As we walked toward the gallery entrance, suddenly I found it hard to breathe.

There, in the front window sat a massive canvas with a photograph of the view out from Ridgedale—across the vines and out towards the city.

My photograph.

Sat in the window of one of the most prestigious galleries in Auckland.

Down the bottom right-hand corner sat a small orange sticker. I'd been in enough galleries to know what that meant.

"Someone's bought it," I said.

Then I looked at Harry. "You've bought it?"

He shook his head in the negative. "No. Not me. But whoever has bought it has an eye for a good photograph."

"It's a one of a kind," he explained. "Frederick likes to handle exclusive works, so I've said that I won't make any more of the images available. Whoever purchases from your show will be purchasing a one of a kind work."

He leaned in and whispered. "But I have bought one of the ones inside."

He'd already paid for the work, the money was in my bank account. For the life of me I couldn't understand why he'd pay for it again.

Then we walked in the door.

If I thought I was overwhelmed by the window display, I couldn't begin to describe what I felt as I gazed at my work presented on the lit walls of the gallery proper.

We walked in silence as images that I'd believed would be used in brochures and advertising for the Vineyard, or by Fish & Bird adorned the grey brick walls of the gallery.

As we progressed through the display, I couldn't help but catch sight of the prices on the work. Tiny prints were marked at $300 to $500. I couldn't imagine anyone parting with money like that for my work.

Further down, towards the centre of the gallery the size of the prints increased, together with the cost. I gasped out loud when a shot of the sculptures at the front of the vineyard came with a price tag of $3,000.

"No-one will buy that," I whispered to Harry.

"They will, believe me," he replied with conviction.

As we turned the corner and moved into the centre of the exhibition, I stopped and stared.

There in front of us sat a picture of the red boat shed at Spindle Bay. A price tag of $25,000 sitting underneath it.

On the edge of the frame sat a tiny orange sticker.

My mouth fell open and I looked at Harry.

"I bought it for you," he said, his hand slipping around my waist.

"Why?"

"Because it's beautiful," he said and as his lips slipped across mine he added, "and so are you."

I didn't know what to say.

No-one had ever purchased my work before.

Mum and Dad had hung it on the walls at the bach, but I thought they were just being parents. The idea that anyone— even Harry Pearson—would pay so much money for a photograph that I took seemed beyond belief.

"I can't possibly accept this kind of gift," I said trying to get my head around what Harry had done. "Besides," I added, "I'm going away. You have my resignation. My tickets are bought and paid for."

Harry waved his hand in the air as if he were swatting away a mosquito that I couldn't quite see. "If you do decide that you're going to leave, you can call it a going away present."

It was the first time that he'd acknowledged that I was going away.

"But we can talk about that later. I have another surprise for you," Harry said his eyes gleaming with mischief.

"What?"

Before he could answer, Frederick arrived. "Ah, this must be the photographer herself." He reached out and took my hand, raising my knuckles to his lips. "You are indeed a most talented artist, Miss Richards. I can't believe that you haven't been snapped up for a show before now."

I could feel the heat rushing to my face. It was one thing to have Harry making promising noises about my photographs, but Frederick himself. That was quite another matter.

"Thank you," I stuttered. "I can't believe how quickly you put this all together."

Not exactly a short man, but stood next to the bulk of Harry's body, Frederick seemed more on the wide side than may well have particularly been the case.

With his thin, dark moustache and his bright red bow tie, he looked even more eccentric than I had been lead to believe he might be.

Frederick turned his attention to Harry. "I have spoken to the Dean of the art school. He's looking forward to meeting with you both this afternoon."

"I beg your pardon?" *We were meeting with the Dean of the art school?* Had I heard correctly.

Harry turned to me, "My other surprise. With the recommendation that Frederick is giving you, I took the liberty of arranging a meeting with the Dean."

Frederick looked first from Harry and then to me, then back to Harry. "My apologies my dear friend for spoiling your surprise."

Harry dismissed the apology with a lift of his shoulder. "We wouldn't have the meeting if it weren't for your connection to the art school."

And I wonder how much Harry has agreed to donate to the school? Asked that familiar little voice in my head.

"Talent like yours," Frederick said again turning in my direction, "deserves to be nurtured. I'm certain that we will have no trouble whatsoever selling the entire collection that's on display here. You'll have patrons wishing to commission work in no time at all."

I could see what Harry was trying to do here. "This doesn't change anything," I said to him.

"Really?" he said as he arched an eyebrow.

We both knew it changed everything—but I wasn't about to give him the satisfaction of admitting that.

CHAPTER 25

*H*arry

It didn't take a genius to know that I'd done the right thing.

The look on Grace's face as we walked away from the Dean's office told me that I was exceptionally close to keeping her in New Zealand.

There was only one other matter that had to be settled between the two of us.

"How much did you have to donate to the school?" Grace asked as we pulled away from the red brick building that housed Auckland's art school.

"It doesn't matter," I said. "I told you this morning, money is not an issue and I meant it."

"What is an issue?"

"Making sure that you don't leave the Island."

"And you think that putting on a show and getting me into art school is the way to do that?" The tone of her voice disturbed me. The sentence was clipped. The words harsh.

"It isn't?"

I glanced sideways and saw Grace shaking her head. "You have no idea."

"Enlighten me." Hadn't I just given her everything that she wanted? "You don't need to go to Europe to study. You can study here. The money you'll earn from the sale of your work in the next few days will pay your tuition fees and if it doesn't, well I'll cover the balance."

"It's not just about the money."

"It's always about the money, Grace. Everything else is just bullshit."

"You don't get it." Grace folded her arms across her chest.

"Explain it to me." I had no idea why we were having this argument. Logic said that I'd given Grace everything that she wanted and needed.

"I don't want to be dependant on you."

"You're not dependant on me. In fact, you're your own woman. You have the ability to make your own money and you have the ability to further your studies. What else do you need?"

"There's the small matter of accommodation."

"You'll be moving in with me."

"Seriously," Grace said looking at me as if I'd just suggested that she should live under a bridge, not in one of the most expensive homes in Auckland. "I don't want to talk about this right now."

"You're right," I said. "You've had a lot to think about today." Besides, we were going to have plenty to talk about once we got back to the Island.

Grace busied herself staring out of the window and avoiding any more attempts at conversation.

The return trip to the Island was quick and uneventful. I decided to leave her to her own thoughts and it was only after we stowed the boat in the boat shed that Grace seemed in any state to discuss matters.

I watched with fascination as she ran her fingers over the old red doors. It looked as if her thoughts were anywhere else except where we both stood.

"It is the most beautiful photograph," I said, "and it wasn't until I saw it that I came to understand how much the old shed means to me."

Grace looked at me with her green eyes turning almost the colour of the ocean in the light.

"But it won't be here for much longer," she said, "if you get your way and you put a wharf here." I could see the pain of loss that hid behind those eyes. Grace ran her fingers along the old wooden rail as if she were somehow trying to imprint the memory of the building in her body.

"That's one of the other things that I wanted to tell you."

I leaned up against the door, the caress of the wood reminding me how long this solid building had been a part of my life. "After I saw your work and I thought about what you had to say, I decided that I'm not going ahead with the wharf plans. I've instructed my engineers to look for another more suitable site."

"What if there isn't one?" Concern etched Grace's brow. I didn't like the look of worry on her face. I wanted to make sure that she never had anything to worry about ever again.

"There will be another site that's more suitable." I leaned in. I wanted to close the space between me and Grace. Taste her lips. See if they had the same sheen of salt on them from our trip that sat on my own.

Instead, I ran my fingers along the soft skin of her cheek. She reflected the action and her hand slipped to my face.

"Kiss me," she said. Had she been able to read my mind?

I didn't need to be asked twice. I slipped my lips over Grace's. The kiss was chaste, tender almost and her lips did taste of salt.

"Do you have any more surprises for me?" Grace asked

when our lips finally parted.

"Just one, but you have to promise me that you're not going to leave."

Grace shook her head. "No, not until you tell me what other part of my life you're attempting to manage."

"Fair enough." I knew that I'd probably backed down too soon, but it had been a huge day for both of us and all I wanted to do now was ensure that Grace cancelled her flights and agreed to stay here on the Island.

"Let me walk you home," I said as I took Grace's hand and turned to walk us both down the beach to the familiar yellow bach on the foreshore at Spindle Bay.

*G*race

There was something soothing in the action of walking down the beach hand-in-hand with Harry.

We passed all the familiar landmarks, but for some reason today I looked at the entire beach with a new set of eyes.

It had been a whirlwind kind of day.

This morning I'd gone to work determined that Harry would accept my resignation and by this afternoon, I had a show in one of the most prestigious galleries in Auckland, the promise of a place at art school and Harry had not only told me that he wanted me to move in with him, but he'd also conceded that he would no longer pursue the building of a wharf at the northern point of Spindle Bay.

My head spun and it wasn't simply because I was walking down my beach with a man that I'd thoroughly fallen in love with.

There still remained, though, the nagging reason that I'd come to Spindle Bay all those months ago.

To escape my failures and lick my wounds.

Surely, the success of a show that I hadn't even known I'd

be having until this morning would wipe away my past failures?

Hadn't Harry managed to achieve for me in what seemed like record time everything that I'd wanted to achieve for myself by going to Europe?

But what of leaving Spindle Bay?

Never mind the thought of leaving Harry.

The idea of getting on a plane in a couple of weeks now seemed ridiculous.

What were my parents going to say? They'd always known that my living at Spindle Bay wasn't permanent—not that anyone ever used the bach anymore. If I wasn't in the country, what would happen to the old home?

I hadn't wanted to admit it to anyone—especially myself, but I'd developed a love of the old bach and the idea of it not being here hurt. It probably hurt almost as much as the thought of leaving Harry.

How had I gotten myself into this position? And how had Harry known what I really needed? All of these thoughts tumbled through my mind as we walked the familiar beach-front hand-in-hand.

A sense of belonging and peace settled over me that I'd been trying to avoid since I unlocked the door of the bach all those months ago.

"You haven't said a word since we left the boat shed," Harry said as we ambled up onto the deck. The new boards that Harry had installed looked so out of place alongside the old, bleached wood of the railings.

"I was thinking about what my parents were going to say about the show and about me staying on Hauraki Island." I looked at the new decking again, "And how I'm ever going to explain the alterations that have happened around here."

I unlocked the deadbolts that Harry had insisted on having fitted and let us both into the house.

"What if I told you that they wouldn't care about the alterations?" Harry said as he sat himself down in the window seat across from the dining table.

"Is this another one of your surprises?"

The grin on his face answered my question.

"What else have you been up to today?" I should be angry with him, but today had been like the best kind of Christmas and the surprises just kept coming.

Harry pulled a couple of pieces of paper from the inside of the oilskin vest that he put on after we left the boathouse and held them out to me.

"Take a look," he said dangling the pages in front of me.

With a tinge of trepidation and wondering what the hell else he could have in store for me, I took the pages from Harry's hand and scanned them.

"It's a contract," I said as my eyes settled on the first line that read, *Agreement for Sale and Purchase of Land.*

The seller was my mother and the purchaser was Harry.

I recognised her signature at the bottom of the paper.

It didn't make any sense.

"You've bought this house?" The words came out as a whisper. I couldn't believe that my mum would give in and sell the house to Harry. "But Mum said she'd never sell it to you."

"Read the next page," Harry said.

My hands shook as I turned to the next page of the agreement. The first thing I saw was Mum's signature at the end of the page again.

It still didn't make any sense to me.

I looked toward Harry for some kind of explanation.

"What's going on?"

"Read the documents," he replied his voice had a soft edge to it. He used the same tone of voice he'd used with me when we were in bed together.

Something about what I was reading and the way Harry was behaving didn't make sense.

The more I tried to read the words on the page, the more they seemed to run together and become illegible.

My insides felt as if they were going to curdle. I couldn't imagine why mum would relent after all these years and sell the house to Harry. And why now? Maybe I had made the right decision booking a plane out of here. I couldn't imagine Spindle Bay without the old bach on the waterfront.

I took a deep breath. Closed my eyes and tried to calm down.

When I opened them again, Harry was standing by my side, a concerned look on his face.

"It's okay," he said slipping an arm around me.

"I still can't believe that she'd sell the house to you." Panic clawed at me. "That she'd let you bowl the house and destroy her gardens and turn this site into another…" I couldn't find the words.

"It's okay," Harry soothed. "The second page that your mum's signed. It's an acknowledgment that I've purchased the property but that it's on the basis that I've purchased it as a bare trustee for you. There's an agreement on the first page that a covenant will be put in place on the land and the surrounding beachfront land that we own preventing anyone from ever building a wharf at the headland."

I still didn't understand.

"I've bought the house off your mum for you," Harry urged, as if by force of will he could make me understand. "I've signed the contract, but the house will be transferred into your name—or into the name of a Trust for the benefit of you. And a covenant will go in place to prevent the building of a wharf. Spindle Bay will never be changed again."

The bach was mine? Mum was selling it to me, but Harry was paying her for it. Spindle Bay is saved.

"But what about Cory and Beverley?"

"You said yourself, your brother's overseas, your sister has her lake house. Your mum checked with them before she signed the documents. She tells me that you're the one in the family who loves this place, so it's only right that you should own it."

I could scarcely come to terms with what Harry was saying. It made sense, but I still couldn't believe what was happening.

"You'd buy this house, for me?" I whispered. I could feel the tears beginning to prickle at my eyes.

He nodded.

I needed to sit down. I made my way to the window seat that Harry had just vacated.

So much had happened today. Staying on my feet a moment longer wasn't an option.

"But what about you saying today that I was coming to live with you?"

"You can come and live with me any time you want. But I know how much you love being here. I only had to watch you when you were here to see the love you have for this house and for Spindle Bay. My only concern has been your safety here and I've dealt with that."

He was right, of course—and he'd dealt with so many things.

Tears began to slip silently down my face. How had I ever thought I could leave Spindle Bay?

"You've thought of everything."

Harry shrugged. "It's what I do. I decide I want something and I go after it."

And he'd decided that he wanted me.

My life had changed so much in the last twenty-four

hours I could scarcely get my head around things.

I leaned back against the familiar wooden window frame. I'd loved sitting here as a child. This seat had seen so many changes in my life and here it was today—witness to another.

Harry sat beside me and then pulled me into his lap. I was too overwhelmed to resist him.

Maybe that had been his plan all along.

"Happy?" he asked.

I nodded.

Harry stroked my hair and I rested my head against his chest, the soft sound of his regular heart beat lulling me into a somnolent state.

"You know what?" Harry asked.

"What?" I was enjoying the sense of security being here with Harry was giving me.

"I couldn't let you go to Europe because I love you."

If he'd told me that earlier, I would have been terrified, but now I was so happy to hear those words.

"I love you too," I said, and I meant it. I hadn't said those words to anyone other than my family and now Harry would be my family. He'd shown me in so many ways what I meant to him.

"This will be our home away from home," Harry said as he lifted my chin, "and we'll go to Europe any time you want. Together."

"I'd like that."

He slipped his lips over mine and nothing else mattered.

*H*arry
Late that night, I carried Grace to her bedroom in the bach. It was the first time that I'd stayed down here and I knew it wouldn't be the last.

We made love that night. Soft, sensual, fluid love. The

kind of physical love that I'd been looking for for such a long time that I'd begun to believe it didn't exist.

I'd found it with my Grace, the woman that I wanted to be with me for the rest of my life. The woman whom I wanted to stand by my side, the way my mother had stood by my father's side for so many years.

The sun rose on another day at Spindle Bay and Grace stirred in my arms.

"What time is it?" she asked.

"I have no idea," I said, as I pushed my hard cock into the small of her back.

"Is it that time again?" she giggled. The sound of her laughter was something that I wanted to greet me in the morning every day.

"Soon," I promised her, "but I want to ask you something first."

She turned over, her face flushed with sleep, her long blonde hair laying like silken straw across her pillow.

"What?"

"I want to wake up with you every morning. No matter what it takes. I'll move down here if that's what you want." I carried on with the rest of the sentence before she had a chance to object. "I want you to help me develop the vineyard. We'll put together a sustainable plan. I need you, Grace."

I covered her mouth with a kiss. A slow, sensual kiss while she had a chance to think about the words that I'd just said.

"You want me to go to art school and help you with your business?" she asked matter-of-factly. I didn't expect anything less from the Grace that I'd grown to love.

"Of course, I'll have to hire another assistant," I said, "I'm sure mother will have someone in mind who can help. But I suspect that any new assistant she sends my way will be male." Kathryn had a knack for knowing exactly what I needed and she had been spot on with the woman who lay in my arms this morning.

Grace laughed, the sound filling the snug bedroom. I knew that this bach had been witness too much family laughter and I wanted to make sure that it remained that way.

"Make me the happiest man on Hauraki Island and marry me, Grace." The words were out of my mouth before I had a chance to think about them. They were the words that I'd been holding onto. I was terrified of scaring Grace away—I'd presented her with so many changes in the last twenty-four hours, I'd promised myself that I wouldn't ask that question, but now the words were out. I couldn't take them back.

Grace lay back on the pillow. Not saying a word. As if she were contemplating a future with me—a life together on the Island that I knew she'd been so determined to escape.

I held my breath. Willing her to say the one little word that would make me the happiest man in the world.

The silence lingered on, the only sounds coming from the whirling gulls that flew across the beachfront.

"Say yes, damn it," a man of action, I couldn't stand the agonising wait any longer.

She turned to me without lifting her head from the pillow, a look of mischief in those eyes that carried the colour of the vines on the headland above us. "Yes," she said, "but on one condition."

"Anything," I replied. My entire body sagged back into the mattress with relief. I would give Grace the world if she'd stay here with me.

"I want to get married in front of the old red boat shed."

Is that all?

"It's a deal," I said and I knew it was the best deal I'd ever made in my life.

ABOUT THE AUTHOR

Hello from Auckland, New Zealand.

Thank you so much for taking the time out of your busy life to read my story. I think I enjoyed writing about Hauraki Island almost as much as I enjoyed encouraging Grace and Harry to find their way to their happy ever after.

I'm blessed to look out across the Hauraki Gulf every day and it has been a huge part of my life.

If you'd like to read a bonus scene from Harry and Grace, then please make sure you sign up at http://eepurl.com/c6Av-1 and I'll get the bonus story to you ASAP.

It's not their wedding in front of the old red boat shed, but I can promise you that scene will play out later in the series. Once you've signed up, keep an eye on your inbox for your bonus story.

The Pearson brothers are so interesting, I'm planning on writing a book for each of them. I haven't decided which of the twins will be next—maybe we should have a vote!

What do you think? Email me, or join us on the red couch (my Facebook fan group) and we can all decide.

I love meeting my readers (old and new) so do make sure that you stop by and say hello.

For anyone who doesn't know where New Zealand is, we're sitting below Australia at the bottom of the world. It's a fantastic place to live and I'm so blessed to call this peaceful piece of paradise home.

Hope to catch up with you soon.

Until then, take care.

Love Toni x

For more information about Toni Kenyon:

www.tonikenyon.com

toni@tonikenyon.com

ALSO BY TONI KENYON

PRIVATE LOVE IN A PUBLIC PLACE

Mags O'Brien lives on the alcohol-soaked, drug-enhanced concert circuit, managing out-of-control rocker Julian MacAvoy. She helps him spread his musical gospel to his adoring followers, despite the fast-spinning turnstile on his bedroom door, and the broken hearts he leaves in his wake.

Mags believes she's immune to Julian's magnetic personality but when controversy hits the tour, she finds herself in danger of falling at his feet, slave to his appetites and her own desire and need.

Julian refuses to be tamed, but the pressure of the ravenous crowds clamps tighter and tighter around him. His chaotic world starts to crumble when he realises his motivation to continue touring comes from an unobtainable woman. Can he force her to make the agonising choice between himself and her estranged husband?

An erotic and candid look at life on the road.

Download your copy Private Love in a Public Place

Praise for PRIVATE LOVE IN A PUBLIC PLACE

I'm a huge fan of Rock&Roll love stories.This one rates right up there with Olivia Cunning's "Sinners" & "Sole Regret" and "FitzWilliam Darcy". I can't wait for the 2nd book to come out in April! This story has it all... Heartbreak, Steamy but Very Real love and really tough choices. At one point, I cried like a baby and in the next, I was yelling at my KindleFire. LoL...

Bottom line- Totally worth adding this book to your collection!

Sexy and gritty, raw and engaging, "Private Love in a Public Place" takes you on a personal behind-the-scenes tour of a rock star's life on the road from the perspective of his manager, a woman who loves the artist as much as she loves the man himself. ... This is a fresh, steamy and surprising love story guaranteed to entertain!

Mags is open and real, a woman I could relate too in a job many of us would see as glamorous (manager to a rock star or babysitter perhaps) but which she made very real, faults and all. Jules is that mix of arrogant tosser and little boy lost, who you can't help but fall in love with. A rock star who shows us he's human.

Other work from Toni Kenyon

CATCH

Tamsen Parsons is happy with her wacky world. So she leases fish to big business, her bedroom resembles a gypsy fortune-teller's caravan and she's got the flat-mate from hell. Still, the sun's shining and she can smile.

That is until uptight lawyer Matthew Solomon breaks into her serene world. He's over the corporate climb, unsure what he wants in life anymore and the sexy and aloof Tamsen looks like just the sort of short-term tonic he needs.

What Matt doesn't count on is his interfering mother, Tamsen's out-of-control best friend and falling in love.

Can a gypsy-fish-minder really bring this bad-boy to heel?

Download your copy Catch

Praise for CATCH:

Wonderfully written and will read over and over again. Definitely one to tell others to read as well. A Keeper.

Kenyon writes a sexy, fast paced, contemporary romance that'll have your heart racing. Tamsen is a terrific heroine with a unique job (nice change from the usual romance heroine) and Matt is definitely a hot hero worthy of her. The sensuality is scorching hot, so be warned you'll need a long cold drink in hand when reading Catch. Kudos to Toni Kenyon for a marvelous story - definitely an author to watch!

This book keeps you wanting to read more. Once you think you have it figured out, you get thrown for a loop.

RETURN TO ALA MOANA BEACH

Ty Carter's an expert bomb disposal technician who doesn't take anything lying down. But a bullet to the back cuts short his tour in Iraq, returning him to a wife who he believes deserves more than half-a-man as a husband.

Lulu Carter wants nothing more than the man she married to come home. Instead, an injured and disturbed stranger turns life upside down for her and their children.

Only Ty and Lulu can decide if the love they shared is worth fighting for and whether they should stay married after such a traumatic event.

Download your copy Return to Ala Moana Beach

Praise for RETURN TO ALA MOANA BEACH:

Amazing book, couldn't put it down. their separation was heartbreaking...but it's a lovely story and shows the reality that many soldiers went through...

A beautiful and moving story about what happens after a soldier comes home. The characters and the gorgeous setting illustrate a realistic and lovely world. Hawaii is a character by itself. Not only does the author portray the returning soldier well, but she does an excellent job describing the feelings and thoughts of his family. The story revolves around the veteran's trauma, but also everyone who cares about him. I love it.